THE GARGOYLES GIFT

MARILU MOSER

Tome Dragon Publishing

Copyright © 2022 by Marilu Moser

All rights reserved. No part of this book may be produced or transmitted in any form or by any means, electronic or mechanical, including photo-copying, recording or by any information storage and retrieval system, without permission in writing from the copyright owner except for use of quotations in a book review.

This book is a work of fiction. The story, all names, characters, and incidents portrayed in this production are fictitious. No identification with actual persons (living or deceased), places, buildings, and products is intended or should be inferred.

Book Cover by Tome Dragon Publishing LLC

First published in the United States of America in December 2022 by Tome Dragon Publishing LLC

979-8-9864261-3-6 (Ebook)

979-8-9864261-4-3 (Paperback)

Editing done by: Samantha Swart

Cover by: Tome Dragon Publishing LLC

Formatting done by: Tome Dragon Publishing

First published in the United States of America in December 2022 by Tome Dragon Publishing LLC

To the amazing group of authors I met this year who convinced me to tell my Imposter Syndrome to shut up and write the story and also asked the important questions like "But does it vibrate?"
Thank you

STAY UP TO DATE

Never miss a book update or new release announcement by signing up for Marilu's newsletter.

https://landing.mailerlite.com/webforms/landing/y9z7y6

Or scan here

Before you read

Your mental health, emotional health, boundaries, and limits are important to me. Before you continue reading, please note there are some darker themes and subjects matter in this book. This is an adult urban fantasy and monster romance with mature content. Recommended age is 18 years and older to enjoy this story. This book contains mature sexual content. There are mentions of death, and a short hospitalization scene in the prologue.

Other elements include, blood, gore, profanity, drinking, explicit sexual content, knives, poison, sexual assault/harassment against heroine *not done by our love interest*.

Tropes include low magic, breeding, knotting, peach play, tail play, fated mates, found family, age gap, instalove, mild praise (good girl), and revenge.

For the most accurate and up-to-date list please visit my website

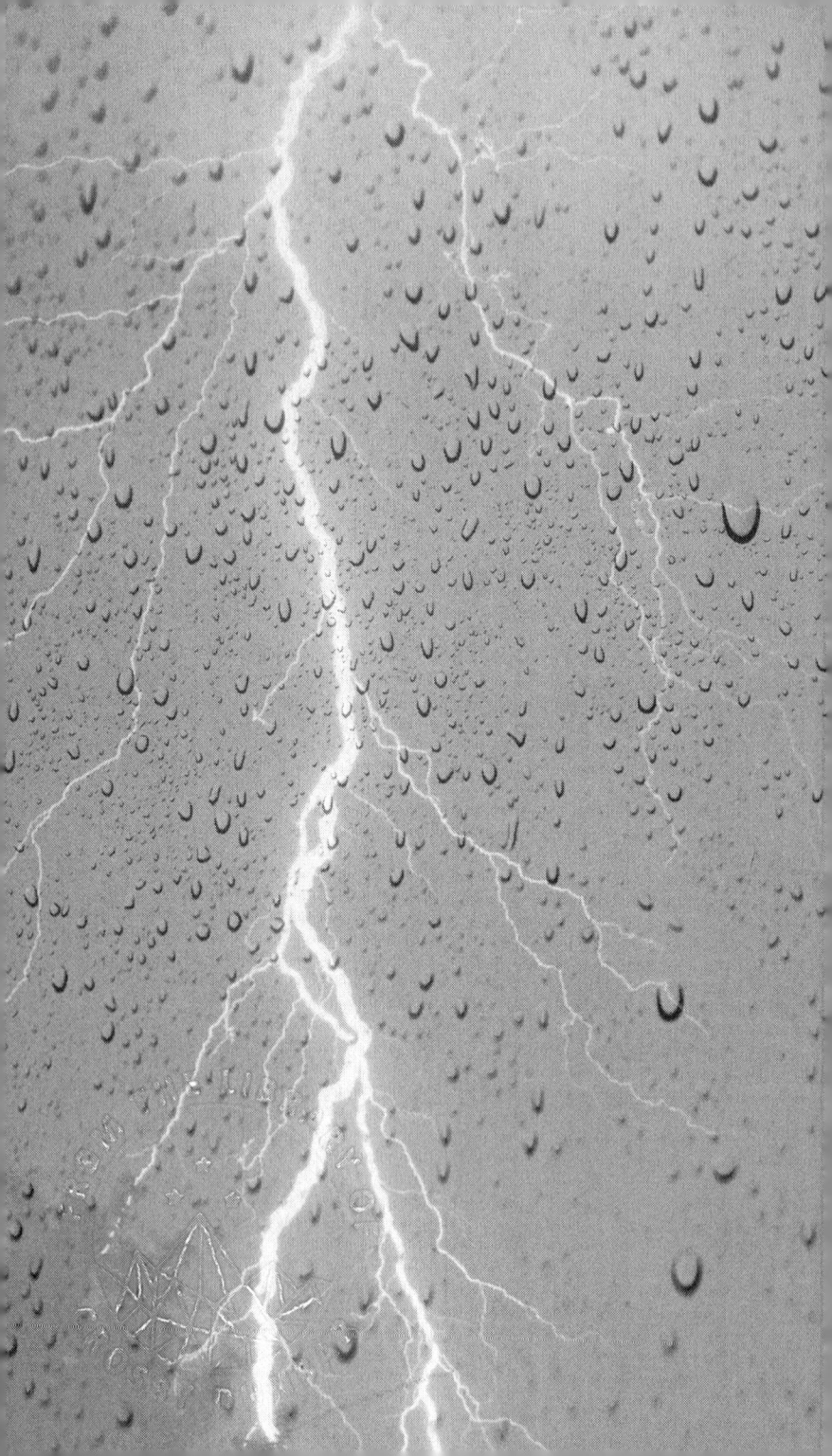

Prologue

The end of Celia

Why wouldn't there be sheets of rain crashing to the ground, accompanied by a cacophony of thunder and lightning? The world is making fun of my current predicament with its own soundtrack. Of all the nights for my brother, Carlos, to not answer his phone, it had to be this one. Where everything went ass up. This was all his brilliant plan, and he isn't even here. Did he listen when I told him to call it off? Or when I told him I wanted out? Of course not. Why would he ever listen to me? I'm just his baby sister, "la ninita de la familia" who has zero experience in being a fucking honey pot.

My lungs burn and I can't see two feet in front of me. If I hadn't taken it upon myself to learn the layout of this god forsaken mansion, I would be dead already. A flash of lightning bounces off the wood-paneled walls, giving me a moment of clarity through the brain fog. My mind plays a dirty trick on me, broadcasting images of the lean six-foot tall man who I've just murdered. I could have sworn it was those coffee-colored eyes with a gleam of red shining down the hall. But nothing's there.

"Celia!" Marcus shouts.

How is he alive? The anger in his voice elicits a quiver of fear through me, twisting the serrated blade lodged in me. More voices echo throughout the mansion, some from two floors above me. Faint whispers seep up from below me. Marcus was supposed to be alone. I should know, I studied him every day. Now he and his entire family are caging me in.

"Celia, where are you? You can't hide from me, babe." The sinister chuckle at the end of his warning sends my heart racing and not in the fun, sexy way. I need to get the fuck out of here. Warmth seeps from between my fingers as I press them harder against my stomach. The hunting blade jutting out from between my slick digets. "Come on, babe, I gave you a head start. By the looks of the trail you've left behind, you've barely moved." Cocky son of a bitch.

The tang of rusted metal lines my throat and coats my tongue. Red bubbles pop in the corners of my mouth with every cough I choke on. When I make it out of here, I'm going to murder my brother. He'll be fine. I'm obviously not good at it.

"If I had known you were this feisty, I would have invited you into my world sooner. We could have so much delicious fun," Marcus's voice carries an animalistic growl and tickles the back of my neck.

Everything is going dark. The blood seeping down my legs might as well be slabs of cement weighing me down. "Ah!" The sharp corner of the banister stabs my hip, jostling the knife more. Despite my best efforts, my knees meet the ground. I don't know which is louder; my heart beat, the thunder, or the front door that was just kicked in.

Hazy figures dart everywhere, there are screams and shouts with a few scattered bangs.

"I'm sorry. Stay awake, keep looking at me. Look at me, damnit!" Arms cradle me back and stop me from falling down the stairs.

"Carlos... I'm... tired." A wet and warm cough sputters between words.

"I'm going to get you patched up. This is nothing. Ma's chancla did more damage than this." His breath tickles my ear before the world fades away.

Bright lights poke at my eyes. "Am I dead?"

"Give yourself a little more credit." Carlos's voice sounds thin. "I'm so sorry. I should have listened to you. Once I get you discharged from here, I'll make it up to you."

Beeping from the heart rate monitor grows frantic voicing my worry before the words tumble from my lips. "He's going to find me. The client won't be pleased. It'll put you in danger, too."

"Listen, this entire thing was fucked. I'm going to talk to the client and fix it. You are going to throw a dart at the map and get out of New York for a while. Okay?" He holds my hand, but never meets my eyes.

"When will I see you again?" He's all I have left of our family.

"I don't know." He finally looks at me. Is that a glassy stare because he'll miss me? Or is it because he feels guilty? Whatever it is, it's never elaborated. We look at each other giving the distance a head-start to form between us.

1

Lola

One year later

Fresh snow blanketed the city while frost coated storefront windows like broken glass. Frigid air burns my lungs while crunching snow under my boots sings out through the barren streets doing nothing to drown out the carols that played on an endless hellish loop at Bound. It's not even officially winter, it's November. Does my boss listen? Nope, he sure as shit doesn't. At least not to me. Halloween was two weeks ago and holiday decorations have already invaded every crevice of Bound.

I give him a hard time about decorating early and frying my brain with carols, but I won't complain too much. I'm lucky he hired me. Lying through my teeth was how I got this job. Did I have any qualifications to help run an occult store containing books on the paranormal, magical items, and supernatural creatures? Or has a healthy stock of apothecary items to go along with it? Nope, not even close. Unless you count playing a grown-up version of hide and seek in an upstate New York mansion surrounded by old novels. Even though I was petrified, I played the role well. I told my brother I didn't want any part of it, other than collecting and organizing intel. My brother convinced me that if I could get familiar with him, I could get the best insider's knowledge and our client was willing to pay more for it. Marcus fell for me, just like everyone hoped. He frightened me, and he enjoyed me living in a constant state of fear and lust. Even if the lust was just pretend

Something was off about him and his family. The weird hours they kept for work made tracking and coordinating their schedules difficult. There was always one wing in the manor I could never access no matter how often I tried with gadgets and hacking. Someone was always there. I'm glad the contract is over, but not how messy it ended. A botched hit forced me into hiding. I messed up and was now paying for it. The fury in his eyes accompanied by the blade he pressed into my stomach haunts me every day. It still hurts.

Howling wind and smatterings of flurries assault my face. Jack Frost is nipping at my nose so hard it's lost all feeling. I wasn't even meant to work today. Javier, my boss, called and asked if I could come in tonight so he could watch his niece's ballet recital. She's the first baby in his family and would never hear the end of it if he didn't see her twirl and leap across the stage in whatever Thanksgiving recital the dance studio is putting on. I still find it strange a studio would do a Thanksgiving recital when usually they're still practicing for their end-of-year holiday recital. But what do I know? It's been years since I wore tights and pointe shoes. Not that I'll ever see a mini me on stage. Marcus snatched that dream.

But hey, twenty-eight is still young and miracles can happen. Right? A puff of white breath filters into the night, taking my sorrows with it.

Clanging and rustling from a dumpster drag me out of the spiraling thoughts. Pigeons flap away, startled by the sound, abandoning their meal or sanctuary. The tiny scratching from a rat's nails skittering across black ice jolts a shiver down my spine. I will never get used to seeing rats the size of cats. My foot catches on an ice filled crack in the sidewalk and my body does a performance of its own for the rat and pigeons. My arms circle wildly while my feet perform their own ballet routine with black ice for a partner. For my curtain call, instead of roses, I'm gifted a chilled kiss by the ground. A metallic tang fills my mouth, accompanied by a frosty burn on my bottom lip. This is why I don't do nice things for people anymore. I always end up hurt. At least the streets are empty. No witnesses to capture my make out session with the pavement, the last thing I need is to be the star of some viral 'fail' video.

Pain radiates up my thigh and there is a one hundred percent certainty there will be a bruise on my knee by sunrise. Especially since I've always bruised like a peach. The hairs on the back of my neck stand on end and I can't help the uneasy feeling growing in my gut. Hiding my limp as best I can, I stand and wipe my face. Luckily, I'm only two blocks away from the Central Rail and one stop from my apartment. My nerves are having a rave in my stomach, and I don't recognize why, which only makes it worse. Everything seems peaceful and safe under a blanket of white and the falling glittering snowflakes. I know better, though.

Seattle, the city where the coffee is hot, because the people are cold, it's a veritable hipster's paradise. It's always busy during the day with pretty people taking pictures and vlogging by the Space Needle and Pike Place Market. CEOs making deals and merging with other tech companies. Couples having lunch at a local park while someone is getting high and sharing the aroma of weed with people passing by with their nose buried in a screen. At night, a new city emerges, gone are the CEOs and influencers. At night, the locals come out to play to see a new band at a dive bar. The night sky flashes red and blue, crying a sad song of sirens. Except for tonight. It's a ghost town and I whisper a silent thank you to whatever deity is listening. I pull my scarf tighter around my neck and shuffle forward into the shadows cast by the streetlights.

Movement from a side street has my fingers clutching the pepper gel in my pocket. My heart seizes along with every muscle in my body. I know that face. Yanking the scarf up higher to hide my face, I look back, but the face is gone. There's no way it could have been Luke, Marcus' best friend. It's only my mind playing tricks on me. He can't find me here. As far as he knows, I'm dead. *Celia is dead.*

The Central Light Rail trip was, unfortunately, eventful. There were a few creeps who licked their lips, making crude comments about my five feet ten-inch full and curvy frame and wanting to see how far up my legs go. *All the way up your ass.*

"Damn, baby, you got a fat ass." One slid his hand across my thigh as I was getting up to exit. This idiot slurring words of promises to treat me better than whoever busted my face only floods images of Marcus squeezing my thighs and kissing each bruise he left behind into my mind. I hope the nerve damage in his hand from my pocketknife is permanent. A little present to remember me and my fat juicy ass by. His screaming carried a great tune with beautiful lyrics of profanity. *Fucking prick.*

Finally, my apartment building is close. It's secure enough, and comfortable. This new home was my brother's form of an apology. Well, this and the fake identity of Lola Santiago. At least I got to create her legend, so getting into Lola's head was easier. I'm an only child whose parents died in a car crash with no other relatives. Not too far from who I really am. Sure, my brother, Carlos, can be dick, but I miss him. Right now, we would be arguing about who was going to cook the entire holiday feast from now until the end of the year. Shocker, it was always me.

The flurries have stopped falling, giving the city the look of a settled snow globe. Panic snatches my heart in a vise grip. Where are my keys?

"Fuck." I grit out after an unsuccessful frisk of my body. I must have left them at work. The keys to the store jingle their merry tune in my pocket. Frost sneaks into my glove as I wipe a spot of wet snow off the building stoop, pricking my fingers like a thousand tiny needles. It takes all my focus to search for the building manager's number and press it without dropping my already battered phone. Three rings and it's sent straight to voicemail. I swear, she is the most useless building manager ever known to man.

It's pointless waiting out here and freezing my face off. My lip stings as the cold continues to bite where it split, and my knee is losing movement.

Carlos's voice echoes in my mind. *"Why are you sitting? Your other leg is fine. Limp if you have to, but don't make yourself a sitting target."*

That's the advice I miss from him. He never threatened any boyfriend I had, only made sure I knew how to take care of myself. What he didn't know was I had already found his stash of files full background checks on every boyfriend I ever had. Then I returned the favor by doing an even more thorough investigation into his girlfriend. After their breakup, he thanked me by bringing me into the family business. Target packages and background checks were my bread and butter. I was fucking great at it. But maybe I should have spent more time learning how to pick a lock.

After trying to buzz several tenants, I realize I am too much of a recluse. Not a single one of them know who I am. Some thought my apartment was vacant.

Limping to the side of the building, the fire escape looks like an option, but given its icy condition, a dangerous one. The backdoor for deliveries is locked, as is the one for bulk garbage. Fire escape it is.

Cold, rough metal presses into my palm, suctioning my glove to the railing. My knee is throbbing and straining against my pant leg. Jumping to get up here, not the smartest idea. I didn't want to waste time building something I could climb onto. Each resounding clang of my steps echoes into the night. A crash screams into my echo, but it's accompanied by a scratching that grates in my ears. The stairs rattle and I look down, seeing everything in place. It must have come from the roof. Two floors separate me from my kitchen window. I already know it's locked, but perhaps stupidity got the better of me and I left it open. Warm breath fogs the windowpane as the cool glass presses against my forehead. The security bar on the window refuses to budge. *Guess I'm still climbing with my fingers crossed the roof access will be unlocked.*

I hate this. I hate everything about my life right now. My lungs are burning in my chest as I finally make it to the roof. It may be a sign to do more cardio, but I will ignore it. Someone positioned bistro tables and garden beds everywhere. It all looks forgotten. The empty apartment is a prison I stay in willingly because I didn't even know this was here. There's one statue by the roof access door luring me closer.

I've only ever seen pictures of Gargoyles online and in movies. My heart thumps against my ribs so hard it might cleave in two. The size of this sculpture is astounding. Even in this position, the sculpture towers over me. He was in a pouncing position, one arm forward with his fingers clawing the ground. There's a trail of claw marks to match the position. "Wow, this artist thought of everything." My eyes trace the webbing of the oversized wings that are shrouding the statue. They aren't fully closed, and it allows me to gaze into its face. A prominent brow, square jaw, and two long, thick, sharp horns jutting out from the forehead. Something overcomes me because I can't help but touch this face. Tingles race up my arm as my fingers go over the sharp features and pointed ears.

"I wonder if you have a name." My eyes keep tracking down. Damn, this sculpture is amazing. Is it normal to be turned on by a statue? Because I'm turned on and not even ashamed. A wave of calm washes over me and I want to tell this statue my story.

Peeking around its wings, I spot the door slightly ajar. "I don't know what it is about you, Mr. Stone, but I think I want to visit you again." Pain shoots through me as my teeth scrape over my lip. "Oh, this?" *Why am I talking to a statue?* Because I'm a sad individual who has no friends. The threads of my glove snag on the dried blood and I hiss. "This mishap is because of stupid black ice. But I appreciate your concern. I should be right as rain by morning... I hope. I don't need Javi asking questions and mother-henning over me all day tomorrow." Can I count Javier as a friend? He is my boss, but also the only person I ever speak to, aside from when his family visits the store to drop more items off.

I feel better talking to, who I have dubbed, Mr. Stone. "How about we meet up here tomorrow? Does sunset work for you? I could use someone to talk to." The smooth feel of stone under my fingers as I drag my hand over the webbed styled wings. Small cracks on the wings pull a frown on my lips. Why does this make me sad? Because I'm pathetic. It's official. I should get a cat or a puppy. Trudging to the door, I glance back hoping that whoever the artist is doesn't take my gargoyle yet, despite the needed repairs. A rush of warm air covers my face as I open the roof door and head down the stairs.

Reaching my green door, I survey the hallway. Everyone is quiet and I'm all alone, save for the cameras at the end of the hall. I'll deal with those later. The lightbulb in the sconce mounted on the wall across from the door burns my numbed fingers. I hiss at the sudden rush of sensation, but stifle the victory cry when my fingers snatch the brass key. Emptiness greets me. It's an icy embrace masked by the warmth of a heater. The idea of a cat seems pretty tempting. Or a plant, probably both. *I could grow catnip for the cat.* It would be nice to have something or someone waiting for me. Entering, I bolt all four locks and do my nightly rounds of making sure everything is closed. As the kettle boils the water for my chamomile tea, I get to work on my desktop. The actual cyber security in this building is a joke. If I was anyone else, I would scam this place and have free Wi-Fi forever. After five minutes, I hacked into the camera feed and spliced myself out of the footage. Like I was never here.

Steam fills my bathroom and fogs up the mirror. It's for the best. I don't care to see how I look right now. Setting my blue mug on the bathtub ledge, I slowly lower myself into the hot lavender and eucalyptus bubble bath. Water and bubbles slosh while I reach for my chamomile tea. The warm and smooth ceramic under my thumb makes me miss my favorite mug. It was black, with a teal skull engraved on it. I wonder if Marcus got rid of it. It wouldn't surprise me if he erased every trace of me. After him, I don't think I could ever have a genuine relationship. Is it weird to contemplate playing pretend with a gargoyle statue? My thoughts linger on that Gargoyle on the roof as I soak. Maybe I should visit Mr. Stone tomorrow.

2

AMBROISE

Frigid air kisses my wings and strokes my hair. Finally, a moment of peace. My clan and I are still working a protection detail gig for a coven of witches. They pissed off an ancient vampire coven by overreaching territory lines and swindling business from them. This went on for months. At least that's what they told us, but there has to be more to it. Especially if the vampires have attacked. The number of witches that have been slaughtered is astonishing. Other covens were intervening. To smooth things over, the witches made a proposal between their maiden and the next in line for the vampire coven. The witches didn't take too kindly to the offer being laughed at. He had eyes for someone else. The maiden, who we are tasked with protecting, had a hissy fit. I guess she's never been rejected before. First time for everything, I suppose. Her trying to kill him probably wasn't the best reaction. According to her, she was defending hers and the family's honor.

Stubbornness from both sides brought things to a fever pitch. Things went sideways quickly, so my brother and sister were called in while visiting our parents in France.

We just got back from a protection detail in Russia. The fae picked the wrong werewolf pack to mess with, and we had to bail them out. I left my sister in charge here after the witch got a little too comfortable around me. She's a client and I refuse to mix business with pleasure. While I'm not blind to my build and how others can find my six-foot-seven frame attractive, I'm still waiting for my mate, whoever they may be. At my current age of thirty-six, I can say I've only actively searched for them for the last six years. I've flirted in the past and done a few other things, but never fully mated. No one has ever taken my knot. That is only for my mate.

Soaring high into the clouds, the snow blankets me and the stillness of the night is too quiet. There's a growing feeling of dread in my chest and not being able to place it drives me mad. Perching on the side of a building, shadows hide me while I survey everything below and I spot them. Vampires. It's odd to find them meeting with humans and not feeding. They're exchanging files, and curiosity has always been my weakness. The one vampire raises his nose. The wind may be blowing my scent, but it shouldn't be detectable with the masking spray the coven provided us.

I can feel his red eyes scanning the perches of every building. Crimson eyes fall below my hiding spot. My wings carry me higher before my cover is blown and all hell breaks loose again. They weren't too happy knowing the coven hired us before they could. Voices below me carry to a whisper in my ear. Shit. Eyes are tracking my flight and now, the chase is on. The clouds turn into white and grey blurs, never blanketing my wings. Whipping snow pricks my eyes, the cold stale air palpable. Thankfully, the moon isn't full or bright tonight. Darkness swallows my form. I've lost all sense of time taking turns and backtracking. Vampires are fast, but only on the ground. Thank the Gods and Goddesses they lack the ability to fly.

Maybe I should retire from this line of work and focus on finding my mate. My need to mate and breed has been in the forefront of my mind. My mate has no idea what is in store for them. Pictures of a would-be mate play in my mind like a movie reel. Spending holidays together, evening flights, perhaps a child or six running around. I have flown too far. I hardly ever come to this side of the city. It's miles from our penthouse, but it's a good thing I was lost in my thoughts. If they tracked me, at least they weren't being led to our home. Godsdamn, I'm tired. It was a long night of bodyguard duty and evading vamps. My muscles ache and my wings are still mending from the tears the delightful vampire family gave me.

I spot a figure slipping on the ice face first. I wince as if it's my pain, because there is no way it doesn't hurt. They look absolutely defeated from up here. There's a perch on an old building where I can rest and watch this show. Even though there is no possibility of this person hearing me, I press my palm over my mouth, stifling the laughter. A gust of wind picks up through the barren streets and the smell that comes in with it pricks at my skin. More fucking vampires. Why they would be near this part of this city is beyond me. They usually keep to their territory. It's too late for a meeting with anyone, and I doubt they're recruiting.

Movement from below calls my gaze again, and I watch as the person walks down the block. I wonder what made this person so talented at hiding pain. The limp is obvious to me, but to others, they may not notice it. Why does this stranger intrigue me? Chilled air fills my nostrils with a deep inhale. This person doesn't carry a creature's scent, they smell human but sweeter. I want to bottle that scent. Then the idea hit me. What if they're my mate? A thrum of excitement outweighs the heavy knot of nerves in my stomach. I want to get a closer look, but I can't without my glamour charm. I knew I shouldn't have left the watch with my sister. I blame the witch.

A flitting shadow from an alleyway ahead of my maybe-mate rouses the protective instinct in me. Even if they aren't my mate, the possibility of the lurking vampire attacking is unsettling. I was sure I lost them. Crumbled plaster burrows under my claws with every dig into the building. Normally, my sister is the stealthier of our brood and our negotiator. My brother is the intel collector and charmer, and I'm the fighter and the one who creates our protection and battle plans.

Rumbling from my landing brings the vampire's attention to me and off the human. I may have fucked up. There's more of them creeping out and climbing the sides of buildings. Son. Of. A. Bitch. *How am I going to get out of this?* I can't alert this human to what's happening. This was all to keep them safe. The only acceptable way for a human to know about our kind is to be married or mated into the supernatural. Light uneven steps let me know the human is close. My next move is not the smartest, but it works. I punch the lights out of the closest vampire. His body smacks against the brick wall as a sickening crunch echoes into the night. Not my exact intention, but I'll take it because now seven of them are advancing on me and have completely forgotten about the human. One tries to sink its fangs into my neck. This one is slow and new, they've underestimated me. I dart my hand backwards and grip tightly to his neck and squeeze until the breaking and popping of every bone, muscle, and tissue resonates in my hand. The remaining vampires freeze as they watch the body flung to their feet.

Taking to the sky, they flow close by climbing and jumping on buildings. Damn, these guys are fast. A roar rips from my throat as one of them latches on to me and tears at my chest. I recognize her. She's the cousin who approached us for protection details. She wasn't to happy when we declined her family's very generous offer. Her scrawny neck snaps in my hand while my talons rip into her leg. I watch as her limp body crashes to the ground. This just went from bad to worse. Two more jump from ledges and claw my nearly healed wings. Pain blinds me and I can't control the spiraling nosedive. Scraping my back against the sidewalk, the only thing left are ruby tracks in the snow, but no vampires. This has to be karma for laughing at the human.

Then it hits me. I lost track of a human who could have been my mate. I'm too far from the family home and don't have my watch or phone to call my siblings. While I heal, I will have to hide and retreat into my stone form.

After circling for another twenty minutes, I found a promising building. Fatigue overtakes me and my wings finally give out. A deep growl escapes me as pain lances like a hot poker through my chest. The scratches are deeper than I realized. Gravel and dirt spray around me as I dig my claws, trying to slow my impact. My heart speeds up at the sound of clanging on the fire escape. I'm too injured to fight and there isn't a good place to perch anywhere. There's a tingle cascading down my spine to the tip of my tail. While I'm curious to see the cause, I know I won't be able to. Depending on how much energy is needed to heal my wounds and recover will determine how deep I must go into a stone state.

"Wow, the artist thought of everything." Her voice constricts my lungs. There's a featherlight touch on my face, and tingles surge through me. Oh my holy fuck, it's my mate. The way my heart is hammering, I wouldn't be surprised if my stone shell shatters before her feet. Oh Gods, I wish I could see her.

"I wonder if you have a name." I hate this fucking night. The need to tell her my name, Ambroise, and hear her say it back swells in my chest. There's a yearning to lay my head on her lap so she can play with my long black tresses. I wonder what her name will taste like on my tongue. How does she taste? *Focus, Ambroise.*

"I don't know what it is about you, Mr. Stone, but I think I want to visit you again." Mr. Stone? It's actually Mr. Dubois, but I'll take Stone for now.

"Oh, this?" She asks. *What are you trying to show me?* Stupid fucking vampires and witches. That's it. I'm retiring after this gig.

"This mishap is because of stupid black ice. But I appreciate your concern. I should be right as rain by morning... I hope. I don't need Javi asking questions and mother-henning over me all day tomorrow" Stupid fucking stone! I want to jump for joy and laugh. I knew the human was my mate. But now I feel like a sack of shit for laughing and not helping. Wait a damn minute. Javi? I'm really hoping it's a brother, or relative, or best friend. I have zero qualms about breaking up a relationship if she's mine. My sister will be the first to meddle once she finds out.

"How about we meet up here tomorrow? Does sunset work for you? I could use someone to talk to." I feel I missed something important. Are we on a date? Going on a date? The way her fingers go over my wings urges me to break the shell. How would she react to me? Has she met any supernatural creatures? Oh, this could be bad. Metal slamming shuts down any further thought I may have. I can't feel her touch or hear that sweet voice. Being alone has never bothered me until now. All these feelings and desires just from her touch and voice. I'm a goner once I see her face.

I hope the Gods can hear my plea and heal me by then. But maybe I'll stay in my stone form and listen to what she has to say. My brother and sister must be wondering what happened to me. They're both excellent trackers and will more than likely find me here. Fear wraps around me like a boa constrictor, tightening with every passing second. I could have just led the vampires to my mate and there is nothing I can do to protect her until I heal.

3

Lola

Mother hen. I guessed it. Since I walked into the store this morning, Javier has been fussing over me. At first, he assumed I was a victim of a mugging, or worse. He still doesn't believe it was my handywork. There's a new shipment of books I need to enter into the system before shelving. Not to mention the apothecary items need to be rotated.

"So, how was the recital? Take any cute pictures or videos?"

"Don't change the subject on me, missy." Javier scolds me from behind a counter covered in jars.

Right now, he's mixing a concoction that smells strongly of menthol. I know he put in turmeric, witch hazel, arnica, and some other things I couldn't place. The man can move fast. He also said we couldn't do anything until noon. I busied myself with opening boxes and reading a book about flowers, their meanings, and associations on an altar. Maybe I should stop by the florist and buy every red flower they have so I can release all the problems in my life and fight all the bad vibes from last night. Except Mr. Stone, him I'd like to keep. There I go again. It's a stupid statue.

"What has you smiling so wide?" He arches his brow at me while his eyes trace over my face. "Stop picking your lip, Lola. It's never going to get better if you keep doing that."

The thud from my hand dropping from my lip to my thigh is heavier than my sigh. "No one has me smiling. I'm not even smiling." When did I turn into such a horrible liar? Oh yeah, after my last stint of lying.

A deep laugh mixed with the sound of ceramic scraping glass comes from across the room. Javier continues to mix whatever he's doing and clicks his tongue.

"Funny how you said 'no one' when I asked 'what', so what's their name?"

Should I tell him? It's not like I have anyone else to talk to, and while he may make fun of me, he's never been judgemental.

"It's stupid, really." My cuticles seem fascinating right now. "I found a gargoyle statue on my building's roof. I named him Mr. Stone." The bags of tea in my hand crinkle as I squish them into a drawer.

The scratching of ceramic and glass stops and is replaced by the slow, measured steps I recognize as Javier. A sticky gel salve coats the pads of his fingers.

"You just felt like naming a statue? A statue that makes you comfortable?" He muses, forcing me to sit in a chair so he can reach my face comfortably. "Interesting. You've never mentioned Mr. Stone before." His eyes bore into mine.

Javier is doing the creepy thing again. He has this uncanny ability to stare at a person and guess what they're thinking or about to do. Then he whispers over his shoulder like he's talking to an imaginary friend. He told me he's psychic and at the rate I've seen him do this, I'm inclined to believe him. There he goes, whispering over his shoulder before looking back at me. "You should keep seeing this Mr. Stone. Also, I'm sorry."

Before I can ask why he was sorry, the sting of the salve penetrates my busted lip. He presses the glass bowl into my chest with instructions on how to rub it into my knee.

"Hey Javier?" I call out over my shoulder. "Are we friends?"

The clinking of jars stops.

"I'm offended you have to ask. Of course, we're friends, Lola."

"Just checking." Can we be friends though? He doesn't even know the real me. I, on the other hand, know everything about Javier Ruiz and his entire family dating back to his great, great, great, great grandparents. Old habits die hard, I guess.

A plum-colored padded envelope slides across the counter, prodding the stack of books I have yet to enter into our operating system. "Since when do you get mail here, Lola?" Javier asks.

"I don't even get mail at my apartment." I state, furrowing my eyebrows. Whatever it is, I'm not going to open it here or now. Sucking in a sharp breath after hopping off the stool, I head for the back room, letter in hand. Shoving it in my bag, I can't think of anyone who would send it. Carlos doesn't even know where I am. Out of habit, my thumbnail picks at my lip. Damn, whatever Javier made is magic in a bottle. There's no pain, and it's basically healed. Grabbing a box of wooden astrological grids, Agua de Florida, and altar cloths, I go back out to the front.

"Hey Javier, do you have any more of that stuff you put on me? I think if I use it one more time" The words die before the thought is complete.

The door is locked, the open sign flipped to close. Even the Christmas carols have stopped. In the dark corner of the store, between the books for kitchen witchcraft and gardening, are a man and woman hoisting Javier up by his collar. The woman, who has a firm grip on his shirt, is easily six feet tall with rich blonde hair tied into a perfect braid reaching mid waist. The man next to her is even taller, bald, with a lean muscular build. His ear twitches and his head snaps over his shoulder, spotting me. He turns fully to face me, and I'm trapped under a honeyed gaze. I mirror the way he cocks his to the side. If he's going to study me, I'm going to study him. A smirk pulls his lips.

"What are you doing?" the woman asks in a soft French accent. It's her turn to spot me and she does the same head tilt as he did. She discards Javier on the floor like a forgotten sweater. "What happened to you?" I can't tell if she's curious or angry. Either way, it's none of her business.

"I had a passionate make-out session with the sidewalk." I try to sound as casual as I can. "What are you doing to my friend here?" Scuffing from the cardboard box on the wooden counter hides the sound of the tremor in my voice.

"How long has this been going on?" The man asks in a matching accent.

"Friendships can blossom overnight, and it doesn't concern you—" I leave the statement open, letting him know I have no idea who he is.

Javier decided this was a perfect time to uncrumple his body from the ground.

"Lola, I'm fine. André and his sister Amélie were asking a few questions about Sofia and their brother." He says peering up at the blonde woman. *Way to blow everyone's identity, buddy.*

Oh Sofia, his troublemaker of a little sister. What did she get herself into now? The stories he's told me about her, always dating the wrong guy, never listening to anything anyone has to say. Maybe she ran away with this guy. According to Javier, Sofia behaves as if the sky will fall if she doesn't get her way.

"They were a little excited, is all. Why don't you go home for the day? You did more than enough yesterday. Plus, these two were leaving."

"No, we weren't" André smirks.

Javier rolls his eyes and picks up a stack of books.

"I'll close up today." Books get stuffed back into slots as Javier says, "Say hi to Mr. Stone for me."

A small laugh leaves my lips, but I'm more curious why André and Amélie seem bothered by the statement. Shrugging off the looks and tense air, I made my way back into the storage room. André and Amélie never came up in the background check I ran on the Ruiz family. Slipping my bag over my shoulders, I make a mental note to dig again under other family surnames. The plum envelope tumbles out of the pocket, falling to the ground like a lonely sliver of confetti.

The itch of curiosity is clawing at my mind while a metallic taste bursts in over my tongue. I really need to stop picking my lip. It was almost fully healed. I've already made a blood offering to the Gods of curiosity, why not reap the reward?

The thick envelope tears roughly between my shaking fingers. Cream coloured paper peeks out. The fibers soak in my sweat as I drag the paper out, photos fall, taking my breath with them. A ceramic square lands on the photos, weighing down their temptation. I know this handwriting.

> "My dearest Celia, or should I say Lola? Was Celia even who you truly were? Or was she just for me? Did you think you could hide from me forever? I loved you once and still do. You left, taking my entire world with you. I'm willing to overlook your transgressions against me. I know where you are, but I am giving you a

chance to come home. Come back to me. I have no reservations within me to take what remains of your world, much like you did mine."

Forever yours,

Marcus

An anchor drops in my stomach, raising a tide of bile and weighing down my feet. The photos taunt me to flip them over to discover what horrors are in store for me. The jagged edges of the ceramic force me to open my hand and reveal a teal skull.

Carlos. Marcus took Carlos to get to me. There's so much blood over him. Royal blue carpet soaks in the crimson river, flowing freely from what looks like a thousand meticulous cuts. His eyes are closed and there is no way to tell if he's alive or not. I know exactly what Carlos would tell me, "Consider it a trick to extort what they want from you."

The only family I have left is in danger because of me and there is no one I can turn to for help. As far as everyone, and by everyone, I mean Javier, is concerned, I'm an only child who inherited a healthy sum of money after my parents died.

Fear moves through me like quicksand. If anything breaks this moment, I'll surely drown in grief.

Choking on cries, my heart seizes. I have to go to the apartment and figure out what to do. Normally, I would talk out the solution with someone. The empty walls will have to bounce the ideas back to me. Unless... The fact that I'm contemplating talking about my troubles and potential solutions over with a statue cements my sad state of existence. What this is can't even be called living. Hiding, constantly looking over shoulders, hyper-analyzing conversations and glances, isn't life, it's merely existing.

Shoving the contents of the letter back into my bag and zipping it fully, I stumble out the door. My tear-stained cheeks burn with the furious rubbing of my hands, desperate to erase and hide my emotions. Whatever Javier and the siblings are doing over on the counter is the least of my worries. Sofia is his family, and I can't concern myself with their family affairs. Running her face and information through my programs would be another Monday for me, but I have my shit to sort out first. When he calls out to me, my feet carry me faster towards the door. Quivering fingers fumble with the brass deadbolts, each clack threatening to break me further. Yanking the door open and blundering into the sidewalk, I let the cold air freeze the turbulent emotions rising within me.

"My dearest Celia, or should I say Lola? Was Celia even who you truly were? Or was she just for me? Did you think you could hide from me forever? I loved you once and still do. You left, taking my entire world with you. I'm willing to overlook your transgressions against me. I know where you are, but I am giving you a chance to come home. Come back to me. I have no reservations within me to take what remains of your world, much like you did mine."
Forever yours,
Marcus

Forever yours,

Marcus

4

Lola

Either this was my lucky trip home, or my face screamed to not fuck with me. The rail ride was quick and uneventful. The trip barely registered in memories. All thoughts were dragged back to Carlos in those pictures and Marcus' scrawling. Racing into the building, the stairs were a necessary evil to work out the nervous energy. The slamming metal door yells into the wide-open corridor. Mrs. Garner down the hall gives me a disapproving look as she hauls in her caddy full of freshly washed linens.

Empty walls won't echo my thoughts. Instead, they swallow the words and kill me with silence. It's sunset, so I could see Mr. Stone. Maybe I just need another face. Pulling my puffer jacket, gloves, and knit hat on, I grab a thick fleece blanket and my tablet. I double check every door, window, and lock before I clutch my keys, letting the brass bite into my palm and imprint itself before trekking to the roof.

There he is, my gargoyle, wrapped in a winter blanket. "Well, hey there, Mr. Stone. Sorry I'm a bit early. I didn't know who else to go to." Am I being a weirdo right now? *Probably.* I guess loneliness makes you do strange things. "You can call me Valeria, or Val, or Vali." The way my name rolls off my tongue is like tasting comfort food. "I'm in so much trouble."

During the time of spewing my word vomit, the moon has joined in to listen to my tale. "So now I have a stalker ex, a possibly dead brother, a boss who is not so squeaky clean as his background check implied, and now I have to run again." *Did I even breathe during that word marathon?*

A gust of harsh, frigid wind whips my long brown hair over my shoulder. Heavy thuds on the rooftop elicit a surge of adrenaline through my veins. What in the ever-loving fuck are those things? The creatures before me sever my vocal cords without ever touching me. They're both imposing at a height my mind can't process. Their stone like skin is a purple-grey hue blending with the rooftop and showcased by the moon's spotlight. Thin membranous wings furl behind them while thick tails curl around their waist. My eyes zero in on the fangs and horns and the rest of the world fades away.

Sound refuses to leave me; my brain is fogged ignoring the plea of my legs to run. Ear piercing screams erupt into the still night, jarring me from my own frozen state. Cracking fills the voids in between screams while a meteor shower falls around me, and rock pelts the ground. An animalistic roar smothers the screams I realize are coming from me.

Heavy thick arms encase me before slamming me into a graphite, colored chest. A curtain of darkness surrounds me, drums beat in my ear. Noise and voices from the other side of the curtain sound miles away. The curtain slowly peels back. Terror should be the primary emotion, but there's only a feeling of safety. Craning my neck backwards, black eyes suck me into the abyss. Every muscle has gone limp as the most caring and seductive smile I have ever witnessed grows on the sharp face staring down at me. *How important is oxygen?* Because I am so far gone and drowning in the onyx pools, my lungs have forgotten how to function.

"My mate." The voice rumbles against my chest.

Mate?

5

Ambroise

Waiting on the rooftop is absolute torture. The wounds are healed, but I'm waiting for her to return. It sounds pathetic, but if she comes back, it will all be worth it. Even if I wanted to escape, I'm not sure what time it is, and without my watch to offer me a glamour, I'd have to wait for the cover of darkness. Would she be upset to find me gone? I would return to her, but in a human form and ease her into the supernatural world. Does she have knowledge of all things that go bump in the night and skulk around in day?

"Well, hey there, Mr. Stone. Sorry I'm a bit early. I didn't know who else to talk to." My mate returned. It's amazing how I have yet to lay eyes on her and I'm already fawning over her solely based on her voice.

"You can call me Valeria, or Val, or Vali." Valeria, Val, Vali. Every variation of her name elicits a shiver down my spine and across my wings. The sweetness of it rolls on my tongue and I can't wait to say it out loud.

"I'm in so much trouble." My heart plummets. Oh, my sweet mate. Pins and needles prick my skin, waiting to hear why she's in trouble. Her story telling of all her troubles is quick, matching her footsteps. How is she saying all this in one breath? Would it terrify her if I broke out of this stone now? Everything in me is screaming to hold her and let her know I'll help her however she needs, if she needs. I can keep her safe.

"So now I have a stalker ex, a possibly dead brother, a boss who is not so squeaky clean as his background check implied, and now I have to run again." Her dejected tone shatters me.

I'm waiting for Vali to give me names. She prattles on with this story, but refers to everyone with titles of how they relate to her. Waiting for her to say the name of the man who haunts her seats me on edge. I'll tear him limb from limb, because she is not running. Not from me. Not from the life we have yet to build. I have yet to see her, and I refuse to lose Valeria now. She's mine, a gift from the Gods of old. Never again will she feel alone in this world. But I need more details about her story. It's all vague and leaves me knowing no more about her than when she began speaking.

Consumed by her tale, the rumbling of the ground hardly registers in my mind. Screams of pure terror flood my ears along with the pounding heart of Vali. This will go against everything I had planned of hiding my true form, but Vali is in danger and my instincts are telling me to protect my mate.

With a guttural roar, I break from the stone encasing me. Fragments of rock pelt the ground. Vali is right in front of me and although I want to drink in the sight of her, my arms have a mind of their own and wrap her in safety. There's a shiver just under the surface of my skin, having her against me. Her frame is thick and plump and fits perfectly against me. I'm still scanning for danger as I shut my wings around her.

"Amélie? André? What are you doing here and why are Sofia and Javier climbing off your back?"

"What are you doing with Lola?" Javier asks me, stumbling off André's back, readjusting a bag on his shoulders.

"Who is Lola? This is Valeria, my mate. I found her yesterday. Technically, she found me after the vampires trying to kill your sister attacked me." And that's when it hits me. "Leave here. You are putting her in even more danger."

Sofia stormed out from hiding behind my sister. I am in no mood for her bratty tantrums. "Ambroise, your job is to keep me safe. Not whoever the hell that is."

"Exactly Sofia, you're a job. You're not her." Gently my wings part and large brown doe eyes stare up at me and I'm a goner. In admiration of her beauty, a grin splits my face. Nothing can compare to her apple cheeks, plump lips, and bronzed olive skin. The way her lips part and her breasts brush against me with every breath has me hypnotized.

"My mate." Her body falls limp in my arms. I guess that answers my question of knowing about our kind. Pulling her lush body closer to mine, an unsuppressed shiver rolls freely over me. I already want to mate and breed her, but now isn't the time for those crude thoughts.

"So, what are we supposed to do now? Lola..." The unintentional snarl strikes a chord of fear in Javier. "I mean Valeria. We can't leave her here and we can't take her. I don't think that would go over very well." He inched closer, and I pressed her ample breasts and thighs tighter against me.

"Feel free to leave. I'll stay here with her." My claw gently combs a wavy brown lock away from her eyes. "She needs me."

A loud snort has me shoot daggers at Andrè.

"You really think she would want to wake up seeing you? Your mate, whatever she calls herself, fainted in your arms."

My wings blanket Vali from the wind that is picking up. "If I'm not mistaken, Andrè, this only happened because you two scared her. How did you find me?" My eyes never leave Val, who looks so peaceful in my arms. I never want to let her go.

Amélie takes this opportunity to recount their run in with Vali at the bookstore. They felt a familiar attraction to her, and now we know why.

After I didn't return home, Sofia used a tracking spell to find me, but all they found were trails of vampire blood with hints of my scent. Then Sofia left the confines of safety, while Amélie and André went to interrogate Javier. It appears they were overzealous. I would expect nothing less from them. But, Javier and André are both correct though I don't want to admit it.

"I hate to be that person, but my ass is freezing up here since winter decided to behave like my last ex and come early." Sofia's voice holds a slight tremor from the cold. "What are we doing?"

An idea comes to me, and it has the potential to backfire. Running a hand over her round hips, the object I need is under the pad of my thumb and in her back pocket. I desperately want to reach in and grab more than the keys, but she needs to know me, and I her. "Amélie, I need your help."

She smirks and tosses me the watch I need. Darting one hand out, I fumble with the watch at the tip of my claw. Vali's limp form sags in my arms. "What do you need from me, frère?" Amélie tries her best to sound innocent, she's far from it.

Cracking ripples out over the rooftop, followed by a displeased grunt.

"I hate wearing this." André twirled the glamour ring on his pinky with his thumb. Disdain clear as day on his face for the magical trinket. The rustling of clothes quiets down as he buttons his shirt.

"Give her here so you can be as uncomfortable as me. Until you explain everything to her, appearing human is for the best. Yes?"

I hate that he's right, but I nod in agreement. Clinging to hope she'll listen to my explanation of everything, I pass her over to him and watch as he nestles her into his arms. Thin leather wraps my wrist while a heavy, gold circle digs into my skin. Magic stretches across my flesh like a suit that's two sizes too small. My wings press tightly against my back, already screaming with an ache. The once pointed fangs and horns are gone. Even the long black tresses have shortened. I hate pretending to be someone else. My normal attire falls off me, and I swap them out for more fitting jeans, sweater, and boots.

The glamour settles over me, and my arms act before my mind. Vali's head is against my chest once more. "Come now, amoureuse. Let's get you inside."

Heavy footsteps fill the night as we all shuffle towards the single point of entry.

"Do you even know where you're going?" Amélie asks, shoving Sofia in front of Javier, who is picking up the fallen tablet, as she stands behind him.

"Javier, walk faster. Any slower and we'll be walking backwards."

There's a tinge of pink on his ears as he looks at my sister. "I was going to say I know where to go." Feeling the daggers being shot in his direction, the stuttering is almost comical. "She uh-um... Lola, I mean Valeria. She works with me. I've dropped her off once or twice before, so I know where we're going."

Amélie chuckles and pats his shoulder. "Good boy. You did a good job getting that thought out." If there was a tinge of pink before, his ears are full-blown crimson now.

"What is this, a safe house?" Sofia asks. The walls are devoid of any kind of life, the floors lack warmth. Not even a speck of dust has found a home here. Maybe she's a minimalist or recently moved in? What would she think of the home I share with my family? Would it be too opulent for her liking?

Scanning each beige wall, there isn't a single picture frame to be found showcasing this brother of hers she might have lost. The reminder of her confession plummets in my stomach. Whether or not she accepts me, I'll do everything to ensure she's safe and knows she isn't alone.

"There aren't any takeout menus either." André calls out from the all-grey kitchen. His head is poking into the stainless-steel double fridge, shuffling its contents around. "It looks like she cooks all her meals."

Javier and Sofia have traveled further into her apartment. The open living room and dining room are sparsely furnished. One small, round dining table with four chairs sits under the rectangular pendant lights. The oversized white sectional sits in front of the crisply right-angled entertainment stand hoisting a giant television. The sides look like carved marble with lights tucked under the beveled edge. There's a pale blue glow over the floor, making the room colder than outside.

"Stay out of her things. We are guests here." The corner of my left eye twitched with the biting command. I can hear laughter behind me because I am being a little hypocritical. My siblings know I'm about to walk through here, tuck her into bed, and learn what I can about my mate. André's voice floats down the hallway as he gives orders to Javier and Sofia to place protection spells on the door and windows. Amélie secures every inch of this place as well.

Trying the first door on the left, my brows pinch, scanning the area. It's an office. Unless she is into extreme online gaming, I don't see why any person would need so many computers. Again, no pictures anywhere. Not even a stock painting. It's all clinical. The only pieces of color are the blue cabinet on the far wall, and the black and blue high back leather chair stowed behind the black L-shaped desk. Everything is tidy, not a single book, pen, or paperclip is out. My mate keeps getting more and more interesting.

The last door softly clicks open, bouncing off the stopper on the baseboard. Is this even the same apartment? Aqua blue and gold marbled textured wallpaper adorns the largest wall, highlighting the king-sized gold, iron bed covered in champagne color sheets. Warmth floods the room thanks to the two gold LED circle lights above the bed. The soft champagne and ivory rug silences my steps, aiding to keep Vali asleep. The buttery sheets slip from between my fingers as I turn them down to nestle her in. There's one large window on the sidewall overlooking the street decorated in art, framed by bookcases sprinkled with a few books, and one full shelf of crystals. Under the window is a mint green sleigh bench. It looks equal parts uncomfortable and uninviting. The longer I stare, the more it morphs into a pea pod. However, some very devious deeds are coursing through my mind, and I can feel my knot swell.

Rustling from the bed tickles the hairs on the back of my neck. Though I'm glamoured, seeing a strange man with a rock-hard dick in her room probably isn't a good impression. Her heart is bashing against her ribs, refuting the calm footsteps coming my way. *Come on, Ambroise, think gross thoughts.* Nothing disgusting is coming to mind. With Vali tiptoeing behind me like a scared little doe, her scent wafting freely around the room and this hideous bench, all my mind can conjure is images of her draped over the edge writhing while I thrust my thick tongue in her from behind.

Pain laces through my shoulder and the sound of a slamming door, hurried steps and yelling echo through the apartment. My mate stabbed me. I guess that's one way to get rid of a boner.

6

VALI

Silk sheets slide under my palm, but never reaching the rest of my body. Light pricks my eyes as I crack them open ever so slightly. I'm fully dressed, coat and all, and back in my room. The rooftop flashes in my mind, catapulting my heart into my throat. Sliding my hand under the pillow, the solid tactical dagger finds my fingertips. Muscle memory takes over as my fingers curl around the handle, resting the blade on the side of my forearm. The room closes in, and my focus is locked on the man standing in front of the window, like he owns this place. *Oh, fuck me. He probably works for Marcus.* Whoever he is, he's bigger and undoubtedly stronger. I could make a run for it and hope he doesn't catch me. There's a hidden power to his stance, and my eyes trace the lines of his body. The man has tree trunks for thighs. *I should not get excited at the thought of him catching me or ogling him right now. Get it together Vali.* Somehow, his broad back fills my view. I don't even remember walking to him. Blood pumps in my veins like a geyser and fight-or-flight kicks in. Tonight, my brain chose a happy medium. The grip of the dagger embeds into my palm as I raise my fist to his left shoulder. With every ounce of strength I can muster, I jab the blade to the hilt and rush for the door.

Squeaking from my boots competes with the blood thrumming in my ears. Swiping the loose strands pricking my eyes out of the way, all movement in my apartment stops. All movement except from me. Those two people from the bookshop are standing out of place in my living room. Their predatory gaze tracks every tiny moment I make. Footsteps creep up from behind me and the living room becomes a blur as I dart to the kitchen. The tall blonde woman stalks towards me, one hand held out in front while the other is holding the man from my room at a distance.

"Valeria, yes?" She asks, like I'm some kind of wild and wounded animal. There's a notable attempt to soften her voice, but the domineering inflection isn't lost on me. Skirting around the large kitchen island, my fingers press against the hidden compartment. While it wasn't on purpose, the timing is impeccable. All three imposing figures inch closer and adrenaline takes over. Keeping the counter as a barrier, my fingers find the throwing knives that cling to a magnetic strip in the tiny compartment. Throwing two quickly towards the bookshop visitors, the side of one grazes the man's cheek while the woman bends out the way. They both lodge into the wall with a slight wobble. I look towards the handsome stranger from my room. Short black hair is pushed back, showing off the most perfect face I have ever seen. Eyes so dark they could be brown or black. His lips are pink and full, and a firm square jaw. Staring at him is like being in a bubble where it's just the two of us. Relaxation creeps into me, and it's startling to the adrenaline pumping through me. Blinking myself out of the hypnotic state this man put me under, I launch a throwing knife in his direction. His hand snatches it out of the air. The blade sliced through the strap of the watch and part of his wrist. Blood beads at the wound. Right now, though? I'm concerned with how this man turned into the beast from the roof and is causing fracture lines to web out across my walls from his wings, pressing against the hallway entry. Holy fuck. His dick is out, and I can't stop staring at it.

A blanket flies across the room and the man-turned-beast, snatches and wraps it around himself.

"Lola! Stop!" I know that voice.

"What mess did you get me into, Javier?" I grit out through clenched teeth, darting my eyes to him.

"You're going to laugh about this one, I just know it." He chuckles while his fingers flex at his sides. "Please, put any other blades down, and we can explain everything."

The leaner, bald man chuckles as he watches me and the beast, who is dripping blood on my floor. "You're very good with those. Who taught you?"

"Yes, she is." The winged creature says. Is that amusement on his face? "She lodged one in my shoulder. That one was hard to get out."

For some odd reason, I feel the full weight of guilt for hurting him, even though I have zero reason for it. Looking around the room, I've made my decision. The legend of Lola has now joined Celia in the realm of the dead and forgotten. Tapping from my boots against the floor gives away my movements towards the door.

"Don't touch the door!" Javier yells out. But it's too late. Purple light flashes from it and I'm sent flying backwards, but never meet the ground. Instead, I'm wrapped in the thickest arms I have ever had the privilege of being in. A hiss enters my ear, snapping me out of my trance. Looking over my shoulder, I'm yanked back into the abyss. Honestly... I don't mind it. I should be terrified, fighting, kicking, screaming, doing anything I can to get away. Instead, my back curves to fit snug against his hard chest, and the rise and fall of my breath matches his. *What the hell is happening?*

"Are you alright?" The tenderness in his voice matches his face. Why does he seem so familiar? He shifts me in his arm, cradling me close. He has the same accent as the other two.

All I can do is nod and watch my hand betray me.

"What are you?" Tracing the sharp angular ridges of his face, small licks of shock race up my arm.

His eyes close, like he's enjoying my touch.

"A gargoyle." He says it like it's the most natural thing to say. Yet somehow, it is. Why am I not scared or wanting to fight? I can't stop touching his face. "I won't hurt you."

The creasing between my brows deepens as I scrutinize his face. *I know his face.* "Mr. Stone?" A small gasp escapes. "My gargoyle."

Mr. Stone's smile is bright enough to compete with the sun. The room is blocked out as his wings encase us allowing only a sliver of light in. The inside of his wings are deep garnet and look like velvet. Long, thick fingers caress every curve, dip, and roll on my waist. "Dubois. Not Stone. Ambroise Dubois. But yes, your gargoyle."

"Ambroise." To be honest, I love saying it. Thoughts compete in a sprint, and one question wins the gold medal. "How?"

His deep laugh vibrates through my chest. "That's a loaded question, no?"

"You already know my name." An involuntary laugh leaves me.

"I know Valeria, but not the last." Ambroise brushes his knuckles over my cheek, and I can't help but lean into the touch.

"Oh, my fucking Goddess! Just kiss and mate already. We still have vampires on the loose." Another female voice says.

Oh shit, I forgot there were others in my home. Wait a damn minute. *Vampires? Like in shows and movies? Vampires are real?* First, I'm sitting in the lap of a gargoyle, and now vampires are real. Shock must be evident on my face because his large hand started to rub soothing circles on my back.

"Shut the fuck up, Sofia. She's new to all this, and they're bonding. We're safe for now." Javier states. His frustration fills the room, but I'm sheltered from everything with my gargoyle.

There's a slight readjustment of Ambroise turning me in his arms so I'm facing him. How can I be falling so fast for this man? What is happening? I'm not one to throw caution to the wind. I need to know everything about a person before I feel anything for them. How is this gargoyle making me feel things? Everywhere. My eyes trace his entire frame and the bone structure of his massive wings.

"You can touch my wings, if you want. I'm yours to touch whenever and however you wish. You're my mate, and I'm yours." Ambroise smirks. Oh, this is how. With that smile, accent, tender look in his eyes, and the way he says things like that. No one has ever looked at me the way he is right now.

Another laugh bubbles up from me and I'm not sure if it nerves, disbelief, or joy. But either way, I'm not missing the opportunity to touch these wings. "Explain everything. Then maybe you'll earn my last name. Right now, I'm pretty sure I'm dreaming." My lip pinches between my teeth, containing the smile threatening to radiate pain to my cheeks.

"Then this is the best dream." Oh, that voice is doing something to me.

Another small laugh bubbles out of me.

"Wow." The velvet texture of the inside of his wings tickles each pad of my fingers and I want to be wrapped up in them. "They remind me of Christmas." *Hecha carajo, I really said out loud.* Wincing at my stupid words, the hue of embarrassment splatters up my neck and across my cheeks and I tuck my chin into my chest.

Husky laughter warms the corners of my lips as Ambroise rests his forehead against mine. He's so careful with his two large, sharp horns, ensuring I never get poked or scratched by them. Three smaller horns poke out on either side of the two larger ones, creating a crown. "It'll be the perfect present for you then." He whispers. Something moves and curls up my arm, drawing my attention away from my lap. His tail is heavy and thick, the same graphite color as the rest of him except for the tip which matches the garnet wings. It's tapered at the tip, with faded scars going up the length.

The second question in the sprint from earlier crosses the finish line. "You called me your mate. Do you mean mate like friend-mate or soul-mate?" I sound like a complete idiot.

"Mate as in soul mate." He places my hand in his much larger one. I relish in the feel of how each callus tickles my skin. "You're taking this well."

Am I taking this well or am I in shock? Everything has either fallen to pieces or turned upside down. I have a stalker fake ex, a potentially dead brother, no other family, and now I'm being told not only are soulmates real, but mine is a gargoyle. Sure, this is normal. Right? Maybe I'm just finally having a long overdue breakdown.

"Would you rather me scream?"

He nuzzles his nose against mine. "There is only one reason I would ever have you screaming with me."

Leaning back, a pocket of space between us forms, but it's filled with an emotion I can't admit because it's ludicrous. His fingers are roaming over my face and body, and I want more of it. More of him. *"I'm yours to touch whenever you want, however you wish."* His statement resurfaces in my mind. Cupping his square jaw in my hands, I shock even myself. There's an excruciating moment of hesitation from him when I press my lips to his. *I fucked up.* Pulling away I begin to speak,

"I'm sor—" He silences me with his mouth. Claws climb up my back and scratch my scalp as Ambroise kisses me tenderly and passionately. This is the best kiss I've ever had. Oxygen is overrated.

Shuffling feet crack this little sanctuary of ours. Am I really going along with this? All I know is, right now, this garnet winged fortress where I'm held by clawed hands feels right. For once in my life, I'm going to do what feels right, especially after everything I've been through. I deserve this. I deserve someone who wants me this much. Even if he is a gargoyle. Ambroise breaks the kiss first, but not completely. The small pecks are just as amazing as the breath stealing one.

When oxygen returns to my brain and all the serotonin and adrenaline reserves have depleted, I'll do what I do best. Create a dossier on every single person in my home and sort it all out. Fuck, I'm going to have redo Javier's. At least there's a starting point. Oh, here's the bronze medal question. "How do you know Javier?" *Way to ruin the most romantic moment of your life, Vali.*

7

Ambroise

Her lips are full and soft; it's the best surprise I have ever received. The way a bolt of love and lightning shoot through me locks my muscles in place. No matter what happens now, I'm never letting her go. She's mine. Is that rejection or fear in her eyes? *Oh, I fucked up.* I didn't kiss her back. *Way to ruin a perfect moment, Ambroise.* Tracing my claws up her back, the slight tremors trekking down her spine thrill me. Needing more of her, I slam my lips over hers. Waves of dark bronze fill the gaps between my fingers as I press her tighter against me. Breathing her in is life itself.

The feel of her large round breasts against my chest, the way her thighs splay against my lap and the softness of her waist paints wanting images in my mind. What would she look like with a swollen stomach from our child? I can feel my knot swelling and I refuse to introduce her up close and personal to my cock with everyone around us. Breaking the kiss, I pepper her face in more kisses as I will my cock down.

This is going better than I could have ever imagined. I'm afraid it'll change the moment I pull back my wings and let the world crash in.

"How do you know Javier?" Vali asks.

That one question, along with the slamming of cabinets, announces the world crowding around us. Pulling her tighter to my chest, I stand, lifting her with me. The desire to kiss her senseless again is balancing on a razor edge. She's handling it all so well. If she falls over the edge with me, I want it to be over the edge of love and glory. Lifting her hand to my lips, I give one more kiss to her delicate knuckles. "That, amoureuse, is an excellent

Pale blue light from the entertainment stand stretches along the ground. André and Javier are pacing. They're locked in debate on who should tell Vali all the things about our worlds. Neither wanted to listen to me when I offered a crash course on the basics and slow emersion afterwards. I'm just her mate, what do I know? Sofia and Amélie have commandeered the kitchen even though neither of them knows how to cook. Whatever comes out of there is going to be a tragedy. André offered to order food, but Vali shut the idea down. She really values her privacy.

"Can you start with creatures? Races? Species? I sound like a horrible human. I'm sorry." The couch dips further as Vali sinks into the cushions, hiding her face behind a tablet. When she finds out Javier and Sofia are witches, and André and Amélie are my siblings, the way her eyes lit up will forever be seared in my mind. Dragging her closer to me, I press her into my side and kiss her head.

"You're not horrible. It would be horrible if you called us monsters." She nods and smiles up at me. My heart races in its own grand prix while her fingers stroke the cotton threads of the pants I've changed into.

A clap breaks me out of the trance her smile has me under.

"Okay, so obviously you have us, gargoyles, witches, and you heard about vampires. You also have shifters, but they usually stay out of the city. Demons are everywhere. They really aren't as bad as you think, but careful with what you say around them. Oh, we have cousins who are Harpies." As André prattles, the tapping from Vali resounds in my ear. "Then there's the fae. Ugh, they're the worst, and I try to avoid them whenever possible."

The couch creaks as I shift pillows around me.

"You try to avoid them because you've fucked more of them than you can remember, some of them related, or at the same time."

"It isn't my fault they have a thing for natural elements." He winks at Vali, and I glare at him.

The throaty laugh tickling my ear makes me laugh with her. "What's your pickup line? *'Want someone to rock your world?'*" André scratches the back of his neck as a full belly laugh leaves him. "Hecha carajo. Tell me the truth. Is that the pickup line you use? Wait, where do you meet them?"

"I'm going to have to try that line." André wipes the tears from the corner of his eye. "Usually at a club just for Supernatural beings and our mates if they're human."

"Can I go? Can we go?" Those doe eyes stare up at me and I'm in trouble. I don't think I'll ever tell her no.

André thankfully answers for me. "We can all go once this ordeal is over." For the next twenty minutes she's given a crash course into who gets along with who, territory lines, what makes each vulnerable. There's also a minor anatomy lesson, which I have to say, was not part of the plan. Leave it to my brother, the wanna be Casanova to push mating upon us. Will I ever admit I'm secretly glad he mentioned it? Never. But the curiosity in Vali and the way she eyed me, I may give her a private lesson tonight, if she lets me.

There's a flash of flame coming from the kitchen,

"Carajo, Sofia. We banned you from the kitchen por una razón. You always have to add magic and it blows up every time." Javier storms across the floor. Yellow light bounces from his hand, snuffing out the flame.

"I'm a kitchen witch. What do you want from me?" Sofia pouts as purple lights swirl from her fingers to the concoction in a silver bowl.

"You're a death witch." Javier says. "Not a kitchen witch."

Sofia coughs as the concoction plumes into smoke. "I'm trying to be a kitchen witch."

"You know, this is odd for me. Learning about your world is fascinating. But having so many people in here is different." Vali says as she scrolls through her notes. Somehow, she managed to not only take notes, but categorize each type and link them with other notes. Sadness overshadows her natural radiance. "I'm glad I met you all, and while this is nice and exciting, I don't know if I can stay here. At least, not yet. I have a few things to figure out first." Landing on the section of notes about vampires, she pauses. "What exactly are you hiding them from? I know it's vampires, but what about them?"

A glassy sheen covers her eyes, and it breaks me. Does she always deflect away from her own pain and problems? Maybe she doesn't trust me enough to share? She's a puzzle to me, and I'm too stubborn to not try and solve it.

"The vampires are trying to wipe out Sofia's coven." Amélie slides a plate of mystery food on the coffee table.

"Sofia's, but not Javier's?" Vali leans away from me, and I hate it. Sniffing deeply at what is on the plate, her face pulls a sour expression. "Did you decide to make coal for stockings?"

The cushions rock with Amélie's dramatic throw of herself. "They're cookies. They were fine until she used magic to make them happy cookies. You eat one and feel giddy."

"That's... nice, but I don't want to chip a tooth, so thank you, but no thank you." Vali slides the plate away from us both, and I couldn't be more thankful.

My sister is still in her glamour, but I can tell it's bothering her. Glamours aren't made to be permanent. She's doing this for the sake of my mate, and I appreciate it.

"I'm not exactly part of the coven. I'm a solitary witch. Being in the coven was stifling. Plus, everyone is always looking on who can be married off to someone and prying about when you're going to start having kids to continue the lineage. It's too much, so I left." Even though there is plenty of space on the sectional, he sits on the ground near Amélie's feet. "Are you two going to keep wearing your glamour? She already knows you're gargoyles."

She and André share a look as he roughly chops some vegetables.

"If it makes you more comfortable, you can take off the glamour. However, you do it." Vali says toying with my claws.

"It's with the enchanted jewelry they wear." Sofia waltzes in with my watch. "Do you know how complicated these are to make? It's going to be awhile before I can fix it."

The burst of magic crawls up the walls and across the floors. Both my siblings discard their rings like a pair of shoes after a long night of dancing. We all share the same graphite color, except our sister's is more of a softer hue. Amélie drags a woven blanket off the back of the couch and half-asses the attempt to drape it over her body. "I'll grab my clothes in a few minutes."

"I'm still waiting for someone to explain the vampires, and why we deemed my apartment safe for everyone. No one is ever in here other than me, especially not without me knowing exactly who they are." Vali says. She stands and my eyes lock onto her full, round ass and wide hips as she walks into the hallway. The sound of doors opening and shutting filter into the living room. Softly padding over to André, who is touching every surface of the counters, she diverts her eyes and tosses him a pair of black pants from our bag. "That's not where I pulled the throwing knives from. Please keep your dick away from the food" She eyes the cutting board filled with strips of steak that are uncomfortably close to his dick and pushes the board away.

He huffs pulling the pants up, slipping his tail out of a smaller hole. "Merde, I've been searching for a while, and I can't find where they came from. I can tell I'm going to be your favorite, and your best friend. Best friends tell each other everything. So where are they?" Tossing the vegetables into the pan, the sizzle and popping of oil mimics his frustration.

"That is utter bullshit. I'm her best friend. I knew her first." Clicking from Javier knocking the burnt cookie on the plate accentuates the fear we all have eating those things. "I'm not the one with different names here. You know me."

"I know part of your life. This didn't come up in the dossier I created." She taps André's shoulder and hands him a spatula. "Even if I tell you where they are, you'll never get them." She smirks.

"Merci," he murmurs, plucking the spatula from her fingers. "Why are you making dossiers? Hmm?" He poses a good question.

Javier's eyes the cookies as if he's contemplating eating them. "Can I read mine?"

Ignoring Javier's request, she folds her arms. "You first." Vali says. Just like that, unease and tension have blanketed any merriness in the room.

8

Vali

The gravity of the situation weighs on everyone. The couch groans, voicing the apprehension of everyone readjusting themselves on it. "You came crashing into my life. I deserve answers." I snatch plates out of the cabinet and they clatter on the counter. André is as still as a statue and the food is burning. Plucking the spatula from him, I start dividing the sauteed vegetables and steak strips.

"A war is breaking out between the witches and vampires." Javier's voice is the first crack of the fragile silence. "Remember how I told you I left the coven? This is part of the reason. I hate politics and greedy people." He tells me the tale of how the witches over reached. "The coven is in the business of creating magical objects to sell and looking for ways to expand." He pauses and waits for André and me to hand out plates of food to everyone and for Amélie to come out from my room dressed.

Myself, Sofia, and Javier sit on the floor around the coffee table. The three gargoyles take up most of the couch with wings and size.

"The vampires didn't like the price increases and refused to pay more. They started doing business elsewhere. Except they didn't stop there." He spears a chunk of steak with the fork and points at me. "They told others about the new witches, who were arguably cheaper in price for a comparable quality." The food muffling his words.

"Ew, Javier. Chew your food first. You're spitting meat everywhere." Sofia says observing the invisible flecks of food on the table.

Long graphite fingers holding a napkin come into Javier's view and wipe the corners of his mouth. "Leave him alone, Sofia. You're just nervous he's going to tell on you." Amélie says with a flat expression. They seem close. I wonder if she and Javier are mates. *They'd make a cute couple.*

The clattering of a fork against the ceramic plate rings out from the left of me. Sofia crosses her arms over chest and pouts like a petulant child. "It's not my fault! Everything was fine at first. We got insider information for almost a full year, but it wasn't enough. We were still losing business. If we lose business, we lose footing in the territory. Losing footing means losing power and influence. There are too many CEOs and politicians in our pocket for us to risk it. So, I asked for the problem to go away. I was solving the problem by eliminating the threat. I didn't fuck it up. Someone else did. Then they have the nerve to demand payment." She takes a hearty gulp of cherry juice, which I forgot I even had. "How he found who it was is a mystery. Either whoever was hired for the job spilled the beans, or the middleman we hired to contract out did. Either way... Not. My. Fault. But yeah. The next in line for the vampires is after me and anyone who gets in his way."

The food tastes like ash in my mouth and once more, my lungs have forgotten how to function. "What's his name?" It's a simple question, yet they look at me like I've sprouted five heads. "I need to know." My plate scrapes against the table and my hand shoots down to my stomach, a muscle memory reaction to what I had to do that night. "Tell me the name!"

Sofia cocks her head back and to the right. "Damn. Why are you yelling at me?" Her fork scrapes the bottom of the plate. Every scrape pushes me further and further into the memory of that night. "Volkov. Marcus Volkov."

"Vali? What's wrong?" I can hear Ambroise, but he sounds a million miles away. The ground vibrates as he kneels next to me, trying to grab my attention. Thick fingers grab hold of my chin and pivot my face. I know Ambroise is there. I know he's speaking, but his touch, face, and voice aren't registering.

My knee bangs against the edge of the table, but I don't care about the pain. I run into my office and grab a tablet. My shaking hands struggle to type in the passcode to unlock my systems. "Turn the TV on." André is the first to move and does as I ask. I broadcast my screen onto the seventy-two-inch television. The dark eyes of a monster stare back at me. "Is this him?" I'm answered with silence. "Please don't make me ask again."

"Why do you have a picture of him?" Sofia asks. The couch cushions barely indent as she leans against it. *This bitch.* Acting on instinct, I stomp over and feel the satisfying crunch of her nose under my knuckles. "What the fuck!" A purple ball of light illuminates her hand and sends me flying back. She aims for me again but is hoisted up into the air and slammed into the cushions by Ambroise.

"Attack my mate again, and I'll send you to Marcus with a bow." He spits out. His siblings are struggling to hold him back while Javier tends to his sister.

"I'm the one who was hired to get the information you wanted." Grunting as I stand. "I was hiding from Marcus and now you've just brought him back into my life. My new life."

Ambroise stops his struggling and turns to me. "Tell me everything."

9

Vali

Three gargoyles, two witches, and one human sit in a living room. It's the perfect opening line to a great joke, and the joke is my life. Did I ever imagine in my wildest dreams I would be told I have a gargoyle soul mate, and witches and supernatural beings are real, and the man I'm running from is a vampire would all happen in the same night? Fuck no. It's something out of a fantasy novel. I also never thought I would tell the truth about who I am to anyone.

The silence in the room is deafening and I could do without the judgemental stares.

"Don't look at me like that. Apparently, we all have our secrets." This calls for the hard stuff. Tossing my tablet towards André, I shuffle over to the kitchen. His claws tick against the screen at a slow pace. Opening another cabinet, I pull out a shot glass and a bottle of dark rum.

"This is impressive. It's so detailed and organized." André sounds like he just laid eyes on a national treasure. I'm on shot number three when he starts show-and-tell. "Look at this." He broadcasts the dossier I created on Marcus, swapping out the black-and-white photo with file images. "It's a complete target package." He shakes his brother. "Ambroise, don't fuck this up with her. She's amazing, and if you do, I will woo her from you." A sharp punch to his arm causes him to wince, and Ambroise to smile.

"It was my job. It's what my family and I did. We're mercenaries and assassins for hire. Never dealing directly with clients. We got work through encrypted channels, an underground job board. It was all based on bidding. Contracts were handed out by a third party." I clutch the bottle under my arm and grab a few more glasses before opening the freezer. The bag of peas crinkle in my hand as I toss it to Javier, who I think is performing magic on his sister. "After my father was killed, my brother headed up the business and picked the jobs for us. We were always given bare bones information. That's where I came in." Rum sloshes down over the rim of my glass as my hands shake while I pour.

Amélie squats in front of me, stilling my hand with hers. The smooth glass neck of the bottle slips away from my hand and I'm left clutching onto nothing, and I can feel everything I built slip away. Everything I learned about Marcus is plastered on my screen. Criminal history, down to a parking ticket, close associates, crime networks, financial liabilities, his non-existent social media, and every place he's ever traveled. "What you see there is a basic background check." The tremors in my hand ripple over my face as I dig the heel of my palms into my eyes. A shaky breath escapes me as I walk over to Ambroise and André. Ambroise pulls me into his chest as

I grab the tablet André holds out to me. "This," the screen blacks out as I enter more passcodes into another secure file. "This is the target package I built when I was given the new objective."

"New objective?" Ambroise questions.

Do I really want to tell everyone that my brother used me as a honeypot and then as an assassin? "The original job was to gather as much information on him and his associates as I could dig up. Obviously, that changed." I can't help the pointed glare I give Sofia. "Marcus spotted me one day surveying his home and took an interest in me, my brother, Carlos..." The images of him being possibly dead chills my blood while tears prick the corner of my eyes. Holy fuck, I'm a horrible sister. I was so wrapped up in the supernatural world. How could I have forgotten about my brother?

"Vali?" Ambroise rubs my arm.

Clearing my throat, I give a tearful smile. "Sorry, um. Carlos tasked me to seduce Marcus, get even more information, then execute the hit." The cushions shuffle against one another as Amélie sits next to Javier. I trained my eyes on Sofia, and a flicker of resentment burns deep within me. "Celia Rosa was the legend I created when I took on the task. There was a full backstory and falsified records to go with it. Just in case someone was to look into me. There were never any hits on any agency or dark web search." The hard planes of Ambroise's chest support my sagging frame. "While filling in the role of girlfriend, this is everything I came up with."

The screen comes back to life and documents containing phone numbers, addresses, work and living situations. Bank and investment records are organized in a spreadsheet based on legal or illegal activity, down to the last penny. There is a detailed spread sheet of how many people are in each location at any given time. After that there's a listing of his haunting grounds, how often he went, and with whom. There's a detailed timeline of his daily habits, along with his family's habits. Every member of his family had a mini file including recent pictures, vehicles, and alias and nicknames.

"This is the target package. Everything was going according to plan. I was gone during the day, making sure the poisons I needed were ready to go." *Because someone wanted it clean and to look natural.* Moving away from Ambroise, I snag a glass of rum off the table. The dark amber liquid burns on the way down and I allow myself to focus on the sensation of it. "I hate working with poison. It's unreliable. I prefer knives." My humorless chuckle is a ripple in the sea of quiet. Knives only became somewhat of a specialty because my father wanted me to know how to defend myself. Small blades are easy to conceal and, if I'm being honest, I find them beautiful and fun. He never wanted me in this life. According to him, I was too smart and too good with computers, and he wanted me in a nine-to-five job in some major corporation. Once he died, I moved back home and found the files my brothers made. Now here I am.

André chuckles and raises a glass in my direction.

"You're brilliant with them, too. You still haven't showed me where you keep them." His statement yanks me out of my memory and slams into the current conversation.

This part is going to be awkward. I can't bring myself to look at anyone. Not from shame, because I have no shame in what I did or the fact that I used to sex to get everything needed. I can't look because closing my eyes is the only way the ghosts of that night won't find me.

"After a night of several rounds of sex and bruises littering my skin. I made Marcus a drink and slipped the poison into it. It was enough to bring down five grown men. Everything went south from there." The caramel undertone of the rum explodes on my tastebuds. "Long story short. Someone came home early, found Marcus and Marcus found me gathering the last bit of requested intel. He looked entirely unphased by what I had given him—guess I know why now." The smooth glass rolls in between my palms. "That twisted smile and hurt look in his eyes as he stabbed me and told me to run is a nightmare I still haven't woken from." Clicking of claws from Ambroise accentuates his emotions. "So, I did. I ran. The best could. If it wasn't for Carlos, I would be dead right now."

"Where did he stab you?" Ambroise grits out.

My fingers run over the raised scar, just above my pubic bone, in a silent answer.

"Merde." Ambroise growls.

I hate pitiful silence, and it's crawling into every crevice of my apartment and soul. Rebelling against the pity and defying the silence, I stomp to the coat closet and wrench open the door. Shoving the few jackets out of the way, I pull out my bag and march back to the eyes of judgment. A sharp smack echoes and the sting from the wood under my palm lights a fire in me. "Marcus now has my brother. I haven't processed the photos to check if they've been tampered with or not." I fan out the letter, envelope, and pictures. "I don't think he killed Carlos. It wouldn't be a way to win me back. I think he's showing me what he's capable of. But knowing he's a vampire who goes to any means for revenge..." There's no point in finishing my thought when we're all sharing it.

Amélie pulls me into a soothing hug, and I let her. We both watch Ambroise pace in front of the television. His wings are shaking. "Go to him. You both need each other right now." She whispers in my ear. Softly, I pad over to my gargoyle. "Well, frères." Amélie looks at her siblings while Ambroise holds me tight against his chest. "It looks like our mission has changed. Our priority is no longer Sofia, but our own."

Their own? *Oh. They mean me.* What's surprising me even more than the statement is the lack of rejection by André or Ambroise. I have a new family. I thought I lost everyone. A smile paints my lips, and this lonely apartment is starting to feel like a home.

"What do you mean, I'm not a priority?" Sofia screeches. "We paid you good money."

Javier shoots up from the couch, and I have never heard this man raise his voice until now. "Aye Dios mio, Sofia! For once in tu vida, shut up. Stop bratting and learn the world has more people than you."

"Oh, my." Amélie chuckles as she pours herself a glass of rum. "Sorcière, has some heat to him." She winks and Javier turns an embarrassing shade of red. "We never said we wouldn't protect you, Sofia. You're just being lumped in with Vali. She's more important to us than you. She's our family... if she'll have us, of course. And family comes first."

Three whole hours of deliberations later, and everyone has settled in for the night, mostly. Obviously, I accepted the gargoyles. How could I not? My instincts told me to trust them and, taking my father's advice of always going with my gut, I did. André and Javier left to get supplies for everyone; clothing, air beds, all the necessities I don't have for guests. Amélie and Sofia went to get magical items and other things I was told are none of my business. Everyone agreed to stay here until we can fully figure out a plan. Now it's just Ambroise and me... in my bedroom, and the way he's looking at me, I feel like I'm a virgin all over again.

"Are you going to change for bed?" Ambroise smirks at me. *Fuck me.* His smile has my panties wet already.

"Are you going to watch me?" I toy with the hem of my sweater.

"Would you like me to watch you?" He saunters over to my sleigh bench, straddling it, flicking his tail like whip. "Would you like to see it again?" He chuckles.

Heat rushes into my cheeks. I've been caught staring at his covered dick. I nod and he holds his hand out for me. Am I about to examine a gargoyle cock? Hell yes I am. My tongue darts out to lick my suddenly dry lips.

"Get changed first, amoureuse." His voice is so gentle I'm unsure if it's a demand or request, especially with his tail skating up my thigh. Either way, I'm happy to comply. There's a tiny yelp from me as he catches me off guard by teasingly whipping my leg. The cable-knit sweater tousles my hair as I pull it over my head and discard it onto the floor. Popping open the button to my jeans, the sound of the zipper is heard over my racing heartbeat. I'm left standing there in a lace pushup bra and panty.

"Come here," Ambroise growls at me, sending a shiver down my spine. His hands brush up legs and settle at my hip dips. I know what he's looking at, and a ball of emotion lodges in my throat. I make it one step and half turn away before he pulls back to where I was. "This was from him?" All I can do is nod and choke on my emotions. It isn't until I feel full soft lips skim over my scar that a tear hits my cheek. "You're beautiful." Kiss. "Smart." Kiss. "A fighter." Kiss. "You're perfect."

10

Ambroise

A goddess incarnate stands before me, and I am ready to tear that lace off every soft and full curve on her body and fill her to the brim with my cum. "Come here." I growl out. She tiptoes over to me with that beautiful blush on her cheeks I know will turn into a full body flush after I'm done with her. I'm ready to make her moan, but she moves away from me, and that simply won't do. Pulling her back in front me, I see the scar from her past. I kiss her in between words because every part of her is perfection. My claw scratch across her soft round stomach. My wings flex as I stand and move us so she is sitting on the hideous peapod bench. The carpet swallows the thud of my knees against the floor.

"Is this okay?"

The way Vali bites her lips and nods has my cock growing and knot swelling. She pulls me closer to her face and we share a passionate kiss. Every inch of her smooth skin is mine to touch and taste, and I will have my fill. Her large breasts spill over my hands as I greedily squeeze them in appreciation and lavish them with my lips. She scrapes her nails over my scalps, pulling a groan from me, and I can no longer be the tender lover I wanted to be. The lace makes a satisfying rip under my claws as it tears from her body and my mouth finds her already pebbled nipple as I toy with the other in tandem. The soft mewl from her encourages further exploration as I drag my tongue across her mounds and down her stomach to where the scar sits.

Biting lightly, the fabric pinches in between my fangs and is torn clean off as I push her backwards. Placing more kisses down her round hips and thick thighs, my hands wander back up to her breasts and my tail curls around her left thigh, pulling it away, giving the best view of her glistening pussy. My vivid thought from earlier comes back to me. *It would be a shame to not play out my fantasy.* I lock my eyes on hers, giving her time to call all this off. She grabs a fist full of my hair and brings me closer to her core and I can't help the grin splitting my face.

Goosebumps breakout across her skin as I drag my claws down her body to her inner thighs and up to her center. Parting her folds, I drag a knuckle up the slit and lean in closer. Using the tip of my pointed tongue, I lick one long line from her opening to her clit before swirling and flicking her sensitive nub. Closing my lips around it, I pull it into my mouth and suck until her hips are bucking and she slowly slides off the bench. My tail sneaks up her leg and toys with her opening, barely pushing inside and circling the outside. The excitement building in me starts a vibration at the end of my tail. More of her drips onto me.

"Ambroise!" Her thighs ripple and tighten around my head and my horns press into her flesh and she yelps, then moans, repeating the tightening and releasing. I keep licking at her dripping pussy, drinking her in as she falls apart in my mouth. I give a small thrust into her with my tail. As she clenches tighter around it, she gasps.

"Do it again. Please, do it again." The vibrations from my tail brush against her walls.

"Gods, amoureuse." I break away from her clit. "If this is what you feel like around my tail, I can't wait to fuck you hard with my cock." The pad of my thumb works small quick circles on her, apply enough pressure to tease but not enough for her to come. "And once I knot you, I'm going to fill you with my seed until I'm leaking out of you." I stand and she looks up at me with lust blown pupils as she rips the pants down my legs.

Her hands freely skim over my body and find my bobbing cock. She pauses at the swollen knot and licks her lips. "Can I touch it?" She asks quietly observing the full fleshy mound sitting at the middle of my dick.

"I'm yours to touch, remember?" The confidence in my voice outweighs the eagerness brewing inside me. I want her touch. I need her touch. Vali's feather light touch pulls pre-cum drips from my cock and more spills as she squeezes the flesh of my knot. My fingers curl under her jaw as she surprises me by leaning in and lapping at the salty moisture from me. She swallows me down her throat, the ridges underneath my cock bump along her tongue. Vali reaches the knot bobbing up and down and working the rest of the length with her hand. I spot her other hand slip between her thighs, pinching and rubbing her clit.

Tears stream down her face as she forces herself to take more of me in her mouth and my cum mixes with her spit as it dribbles down her chin. Vali gasps for air as she releases me from her mouth. My head falls back, and my wings extend as she stuffs her mouth with my balls and works her hand up and down my cock. Every time she gets to the knot, there's a gentle squeeze that has me rocking further into her hand. Releasing my balls, she swirls her tongue over the tip of my cock before swallowing the length. I slip out of her.

"Stand." A single word command is all I'm capable of uttering. My focus is on making this fantasy come true. My tail whips against her breasts and she lets out a moan of pleasure.

Draping her over the edge of the bench, I sit behind her and spread her ass cheeks.

"Has this ever been touched?"

"Not in a very long time." She pants with the most seductive smile I have ever seen.

I'm about to change that. Lifting her ass so her back bows, a scream rips from her throat as I thrust my thick tongue into her from behind. Gathering her juices on my tongue, I spit it onto the tight opening of her ass. My tail vibrates with anticipation as it slowly pushes against that tight ring of muscles as I work her pussy with my tongue. My tail slips past the entrance and I wait for her to adjust to the sensation.

When she wiggles her ass, I waste no time in pumping my tail in and out of her. She reaches her hand between her legs and strokes my cock. I grunt as she works me, harder and faster. I can feel her tightening around my tongue and tail. My knot is swelling in her hand and she squeezes it. An orgasm tears through her and I lap up every drop of her as I cum everywhere, harder than I ever have.

Cradling her close to my chest, I stand and carry her into the adjacent bathroom and start a bath for my perfect mate. Setting her on the counter, I wrap my arms around her, massaging her back while she places kisses on my chest.

"Torres." She blurts out. "My last name."

Gods I love how she blushes. "Valeria Torres. I like it." *Valeria Dubois sounds better.*

"So next time, are you going to knot me?" Her smile presses against me and she snorts as I let out a rumble of laughter.

"I don't know that you're ready to handle it. But eventually," I pull away and cup her face. "I want to knot you."

"This was designed to push babies out. I can handle it." The image of her soft stomach becoming full and round with our brood makes me hard again. "Tub is going to overfill." She giggles.

"Merde." Turning the water off, I turn and scoop her up and set her in the water before I climb in behind her. Leaning her back against my chest and help her bathe. I could do this for the rest of my life.

11

Vali

One full month and four days have come and gone since I met my gargoyle and crash landed into the world of the supernatural. Ambroise refuses to leave and I'm not going to complain. We've had more sex than I can keep track of on every surface of this place. I'm determined to take his knot. Amélie and André tag team watching over Javier and his sister. I'm running facial recognition through every camera in the city, hoping to get a glimpse of Marcus or his known associates so we can end this. I haven't been allowed to leave by myself and while I understand it's for my safety, it's fucking stifling. But a new target package is being built based on the information I'm given. André insists on learning my tricks and systems so I'm teaching him. He still hasn't found where my secret knife compartments are hidden around the apartment. Every day he pushes and prods random surfaces, trying to find them. He can have fun with that. Even if he finds them, they'll never open.

Right now, though, I'm unpacking the surprise arsenal Sofia and Amélie brought with them. There's a seven-foot tree Sofia, Amélie and I are decorating while I my favorite salsa Christmas music in the plays on shuffle in the background. The guys are out getting more food as well as some more books and herbs from Bound.

"How are you still walking? You two have been fucking like werewolves in heat." Sofia laughs.

After our tiff, we actually get along great. Sure, she's bratty, she's never heard the word no, and had anyone follow through with it. She's like that really loud prima who parties too much but will fight someone for you with zero hesitation. Whoever she ends up with is going to need the patience of La Virgen Santa.

"Forget the walking. Are you trying for babies yet? I want to spoil them rotten and give them back." Amélie says.

"Yeah, well. Maybe one day." The cheeriness becomes somber as I watch the reflection of the twinkling lights on the silver ornament. My scar itches reminding me of a future I may never have. "The practice is fun though."

Sofia clears her throat while staring at my stomach. "Well, if it's something you want, there is plenty of time and ways to go about it. What about you, Amélie?"

"Oh no. I'll babysit and spoil, that's it." She furiously shakes her head.

I laugh and hang the ornament on my hand on the tree.

"You sound like Javier. He doesn't want kids either." Turning to stack the empty boxes, I say, "You two make a cute couple, you know."

A crash of glass followed my burst of laughter from Sofia brings back the cheeriness. At least for me and Sofia, Amélie is standing frozen. She's almost in stone form.

Clapping my hands, I get their attention. "Okay ladies, time to try the coquito we made earlier."

"I still say you should have put eggs in it." Sofia huffs as she swirls the cinnamon stick in her glass.

I place a cinnamon stick into my glass and stir, staring her straight in the eyes. "You ever try to add eggs to my coquito again and we're going to fight." As the coconut drink slides down my throat, all the significant memories of my childhood rush back to me. Now, here I am drinking it with my new family, but I can't help the sadness of Carlos missing.

"Santa's elves were busy." André announces their arrival. He and Ambroise are both in glamour. While human Ambroise is painfully handsome and almost to perfect to look at, I prefer him in his natural state.

I notice the red hat lined with white fluff. "Oh my, Santa." I chuckle.

His confident stride has me biting my lip. "Well, amoureuse." He tugs me to him by my hips. "Tell Santa. Have you been nice or naughty?" The brush of his lips against mine pulls a small moan from me.

"Gross. Can we eat dinner without you two trying to fuck every five minutes?" Sofia groans as she eyes the mountain of food the guys brought back.

Amélie hip checks her, teasing her about being curious about me being able to walk. Somehow, I'm the only one embarrassed because even Ambroise joins in saying now he has a new goal. Folding my hands, I send up a prayer, "Querido Dios, ayúdame a mí y a mi chocha a sobrevivir la noche."

Sofia's jaw goes slack before she doubles over in laughter and Javier chokes on his water.

An evening full of laughter followed by updating information on the target package ends. The vampires in the city have all seemed to settle down, but there have been whispers of a new guy in the concerning. What's concerning is that there are no hits on facial recognition for him or any known associates. We all hugged goodbye, and I watched from my front door as they left. André is accompanying Sofia back to the coven house while Amélie goes with Javier back to Bound, leaving me and Ambroise home alone. The pillows surround me in softness as I sit back on the couch, organizing the new files André and Ambroise collected. With the system being new, there are a lot of bugs, making this process a pain in the ass.

The kitchen faucet turns off, and the illuminated screen snared my attention. I don't even notice Ambroise standing in front of me. He plucks the tablet from me and slides it across the table. His arms cage me before lifting me. The room spins as he sits on the couch, placing me to straddle his lap. Brushing my fingers over his face, my head tilts. It's odd still seeing him as a human. "Why are you still in glamour?"

"How do you prefer me?" The vulnerability in his eyes has me falling harder for this man.

Placing a long kiss on his lips, I pull away from him and rest my forehead on his. It's amazing how even under this glamour, I can tell where his horns are. "I prefer you, however you're most comfortable."

How I ended up speared on his cock, grabbing his horns like a handle bars, is a great question. One I'm not sure I have the answer for. Ambroise's claws dig into my back as he bounces me up and down his thick, ribbed cock. Grinding on his lap, my clit rubs against his firm knot, sending waves of pleasure through me. His smooth horns embed into my palms as I pull his face closer to my chest. His thick, long, pointed tongue works wonders around each nipple. Goosebumps spread across my skin as his fangs scrape and nip at my pebbled peaks.

His tail slides between us and pushes into my pussy, filling and stretching me along with his cock.

"Just like that, Vali. Such a good girl, taking my cock and tail in that tight, wet pussy. I'm going to get you ready for my knot. Fill you to the brim with my cum." He bites down on my breast, leaving a beautiful imprint of his teeth. His tail vibrates harder.

Buzzing from my phone becomes white noise in our lust filled haze. "Coño, Ambroise. I'm so close."

"Then come for me." His grip tightens, and a sheen breaks out across his brow. Our bodies are slick with sweat rubbing against each other, creating more friction. The phone continues to buzz, careening off the table, and clattering to the ground. Sliding out of me, he stands and moves behind me, flipping me on all fours. Without warning, he rams his cock and tail into me again. His movements become erratic and my back bows. His large hands snake up my back, caressing and squeezing every curve and dip until one ends up cradling my neck. With his free hand he lands a heavy smack on my ass and the vibration from his tail sends me over the edge. I'm chanting his name like a mantra. A growl releases from him as he spills into me, and I clench tightly around him. There's so much it's barely staying in me and I'm dripping down my thighs and onto him. He continues to rock against me, rubbing my clit against his knot, letting me ride the last of my high.

Ambroise lifts me and lies on the couch, pulling me down onto his chest. My phone moves in slow circles as it continues to buzz.

"I should check that." I rest my head between his shoulder and jaw.

"Let's get cleaned up first." Ambroise lifts me slightly, and places kisses on my nose and lips. Watching his naked form walk down the hall, the illuminated screen on the phone beckons for my attention. *He's finally done it.* There's a delicious tingle from my lips down to my toes, and I don't think I can walk. He comes back with a wet cloth in one hand

and a dry towel in the other. After cleaning me up, he hands me my phone and snuggles in behind me, draping a blanket over us.

His fingers toy with my hair while soothingly scratching my scalp and I hum in satisfaction. The satisfaction is short-lived as I open the notification to see a string of text messages from an unknown number with pictures of Carlos around the corner of my apartment building.

12

MARCUS

One year. One full fucking year I've been searching for my Celia. I fell hard when I laid eyes on her that night. Those doe eyes, model height and curves my hands could explore for days. She was a quiet skittish thing, unless I was fucking her and making her mine. She was mine to play with, and she played so well. Celia took everything I dealt her. Her tears would spur me on. Then she had to betray me. Looking back, I regret what I did. I shouldn't have stabbed her with my hunting knife, but emotions were high, and she tried to kill me first. I only wanted to hurt her a little more than I normally would. Remind her of her place. I can still smell the delicious scent of her blood on my hands. When she ran, I licked the blade clean. Now I need more. If she wants to play rough, I'll fuck her, then feed off her.

Oh, she gave me a hard time finding out who she is. I had to use the extensive network of our informants and soldiers across the country. I'm ecstatic to know she's with the witches my family needs gone. They've been a thorn in our side for far too long. Constantly expanding into other states, and much to our surprise, supplying other vampire covens with magical items. Tsk tsk. Does no one have any loyalty anymore?

But now my focus is on her. Celia, Lola, who I now know, is Valeria Torres. She'll always be Celia to me. Her brother was so helpful in giving up the information on her... at least he was after I turned him. As the adage goes, keep your friends close, and your enemies closer.

Humans turning is an excruciating process. To feel every tissue and fiber in your body become necrotic, then turn undead. Warm, thin blood becomes thick and cold, and trudges through your veins. Next comes the hunger, an uncontrollable urge to gorge on every thrumming pulse you hear. The little shit doesn't like to fall in line. After getting files confirming Seattle as Celia's location, I showed them to him, then turned him loose. He really is an idiot to believe he could have escaped so easily. Carlos may have killed a few of my guards, but it gave him a sense of freedom. It is the season of giving, and I am nothing if not a charitable man.

One of my contacts found her number. My thumb hovers over the green circle. Would she answer? The need to hear her timid voice is unbearable, but I'll send pictures instead.

Why is there no reply? I sent her photos of her brother alive—mostly—and well. She should be crying and screaming on the end of the phone. Screw it. The warehouse is home to local vampires who get high off magical infused blood and fuck whatever is closest to them. Tonight, it's mostly nymphs. The cement walls whisper my steps back to me as the call rings and is ignored. How naughty of Celia to ignore me. Dust and debris flurries around me as my fist collides with a pillar. I can feel it all slipping away as I pull my hair. She better fucking answer. *I need her to answer.*

Thirty-seven rings later, her breath fills my ear, and a grin grows on my face.

"Marcus." My name drips from her lips like fine wine. My pants begin to strain. There's a blonde forest nymph with streaks of green in her hair staring at me. Curling my finger, I beckon her over. She stands, adjusting the skirt around her thin thighs and attempts a seductive walk.

"What did you do to my brother, Marcus?" There's a minor tremor in her voice and I can't contain it.

"Celia." I groan her name. Gods, do I miss her. Pointing to the nymph, I instruct her to kneel on the dirty ground. She graciously undoes my belt buckle, button, and zipper, and my cock springs free. All I can focus on is Celia and her breathing in my ear. My hand strokes over my cock to the rhythm of her breathing. I can picture her large doe eyes looking up at me as I fuck her face. "Celia." I groan again, pressing the head of my cock to the nymph's lips and she eagerly obliges sucking me in and swallowing me.

"What do you want?" She bites out. Gone are the traces of fear. I can fix that. Celia will be docile and laid at my feet on a very short leash in no time. The nymph is sloppily bobbing up and down, choking only halfway. Using my free hand, blonde and green tresses slip between my fingers as I force myself down further.

"You." My hips piston faster while my chest heaves. "I gave you a chance..." The swelling of my cock pushes against the corners of the nymph's mouth and I pretend it's Celia's lips stretched around me. "You had the power to end it all. Come back to..." My release rushes out and drips down this nymph's chin. "Back to me. Come home, babe." Euphoria surrounds me and leaves me with Celia's next words.

"You were never my home. You were a job." The line disconnects.

Wrong move, babe. Wrong fucking move. I'll have to be rougher than I thought. Looking down, big green eyes stare up at me as she pulls her tits out and plays with her nipples. I want Celia looking at me like this, playing with herself for me. Those should be doe eyes. Wrath seeps from my pores as I reach down and lift the little whore by her neck. Her toes are nowhere near the ground and her face turns a beautiful shade of purple. "I'll do this to you, so I won't do it to her when she comes to me." The snapping of her frail bones fills my palm and my finger burrow under her skin until the silk of muscle pushes against each pad. Curling my fingers tighter, I rip her throat out and toss her away. No one dares to say a word to me for fear of them being next as I suck each digit clean. Tucking myself back into my pants, my thoughts settle on Celia.

13

Ambroise

My voice has fallen on deaf ears as Vali stares at her phone.

"Vali, please tell me what is wrong?" The screen tilts, and she shows me what petrified her. The next series of pictures calls upon my protective nature. Carlos, her brother, is standing around the corner from her building. This doesn't sit well with me. Why would he be lurking instead of wanting to see his sister, especially after being tortured? The next picture creates a rockslide of anger and worry in the pit of my stomach. André and Sofia are being followed by a group of vampires.

Grabbing my phone out from the long-forgotten pants, I dial Amélie. My heart is revving with every passing ring. I try three more times with no answer. The phone crunches in my hand as I squeeze out my frustration. I need to check on the others.

Vali's footsteps are racing down the hall and a door slams closed.

"Vali?" I call out. Clutching both our phones. Following the muffled sounds of her behind a door, I end up in the bedroom. She's already dressed in black jeans and a grey cropped sweater she tugs over her knuckles. "What are you doing?"

"What does it look like I'm doing?" She tosses me a pair of pants from the stack of clothes I've slowly started to hoard here. "My brother if that really is my brother, is out there. The rest of our family is in danger, too."

My tail slips into the hole in the back of the snug linen pants as I pull them up. *Our family.* The thought pulls a smile on my lips. The smile fades from my face as I think about our family.

"André and Amélie aren't answering."

Buzzing from her phone takes up any space for conversation. The unknown number.

"Don't answer it. There's only one person I know who is this relentless." Vali says as she scratches her palm. "I have an idea."

Worry spikes with every ignored call. Vali is at her desk, the clacking of her keyboard accentuating the urgency of our situation.

"Give it here." She motions to the phone. As soon as it slides into her hand, she pairs it to the tracking system she coded. The phone rings and her finger hovers, a notable tremor in her touch as she answers. "Marcus."

The next few minutes have me pacing, trying to calm my rage. Hearing him voice his desire for my mate boils my blood and the feral side of me claws to be unleashed. How dare he call himself her home! Home is wherever her heart has settled and feels safe. I can only pray to the Gods she finds me worthy.

"You were a job." She disconnects the call, and the screen illuminates the fury in her eyes. "I know where he is. The abandoned flour mill on 16th." The chair creaks as she leans back.

I try one more time to call my siblings. André once again, doesn't answer. Amélie answers on the first ring.

"Sœur, are you okay?" I ask.

The few seconds of silence stretch for an eternity. "Vampires found us. I'm okay, so is Javier. We're at Bound. It was a swarm of them. Have you heard from André?" Exhaustion laces her words. "Javier called Sofia, but it's getting forwarded to voicemail."

"He isn't answering his phone for me either." Soft fingers brush up my arm, sending ribbons of tingles through me. Pressing Vali into my side, calm takes over. "Stay there. Vali and I are on our way."

14

VALI

Colors dot my vision as my eyes squeeze shut. *Maldita sea este frío.* If it wasn't for Ambroise huddling me close to his chest, my nipples would cut glass. This overpriced puffer jacket does nothing for the frost woven air up here. I'm also scared out of my mind to be flying. All my gargoyle did was laugh at me. Tucking my face deeper into his neck, I clutch my bag tighter and breathe him in trying to forget about the ground below us until we get to Bound.

Ambroise lands with precision in the alley behind the bookshop and gently sets me on my feet. Lacing our fingers together, we make our way through the quiet alley way and knock on the backdoor. Amélie cracks it open and eyes us. Relief paints her face as she wraps us both in a warm and strong embrace, with me squished in the middle.

"I'm glad you're both okay." She rests her forehead on Ambroise's.

"Fragile human here." I squeak out. And her laughter rings out like Christmas bells.

Grabbing my shoulders, she gives me a serious look. "Carlos is here. Prepare yourself. He's still your brother. Remember that."

What the fuck does that mean?

The frigid air bites at my clammy palms. I'm elated to see my brother, but there's an underlying hint of apprehension in the back of my mind. Ambroise gives my hand a reassuring squeeze and I prepare myself for whatever I'm about to encounter.

Somewhere in this occult book shop there has to be a book containing a spell, potion, or something that will either help me go blind or erase memories. If there isn't, I'm asking Javier to create one. I haven't seen my brother in a little over a year, and when I get anything from him, it's pictures of him probably dead. Seeing Carlos with his hand down Sofia's pants made me snap.

"Jodio pendejo!" I shout from the door leading into the stockroom startling him. "You know Marcus is after me." I stomp in and start shoving him. "You know I thought you could be dead. You know where I live." My palm stings as I slap his chest, but it doesn't compare to the burn in my eyes. Is it hypocritical of me? A little, but until a few hours ago, I didn't even know if he was alive, and emotions are running at an all-time high.

"Leave him alone." Sofia tries to get between us. Shooting her a warning look, she backs away with a huff.

Carlos shields his face and chest with his arms.

"Stop hitting me, and I can explain." His arms drop and they bring my heart with them. His eyes look just like Marcus's. Gone are the light brown eyes I knew. Now there's a red sheen in them. Black veins shrink around his eyes, along with his fangs. "I've missed you." He smiles and opens his arms, masking his newfound insecurity.

I tug my jacket sleeves over my knuckles. *Fuck, this is my fault.*

"Don't look at me like that. This isn't your fault, plus I'm okay with it." His face lingers somewhere between hopeful and guilt-ridden. The slap of his hands against his thighs outweighs the sound of his heavy sigh. "I wanted to see you as soon as I found out where you were. I just didn't know how to explain this to you. As far as I knew, you were oblivious to it all." Carlos's hand motioned over himself and around the room. The soles of his boots barely echo in the tense atmosphere. "I finally had the cojones to tell you today, and I was going to, but then..." I traced his line of sight over to Sofia. "I caught her scent and couldn't resist following her."

"I want to be mad at you, but I missed you so damn much." Silent tears stream down my face. He's still here, a little different, but that's okay. Hell, I have a gargoyle for a mate, so why not a vampire for a brother? *What is my life?* My toes brush the ground as I wrap my arms around his neck and lifts me in a bone-crushing hug. "Wait, are you two mates?" I ask, breaking away from my brother.

Ambroise wraps his arms around my arms and chest while resting his chin on my head. "Same concept, but for vampires, they're beloveds." He places a kiss on my head and walks to meet Carlos. "Ambroise Dubois." He holds his hand out. "I'm your sister's mate."

Carlos eyes him before shaking his hand. "So, you're the one keeping her safe?"

"And satisfied." Amélie laughs, and I want to die.

Laughter rings out and I kill the cheer with the knives I have for teeth. "This is great and all, but I don't want to make a habit of losing brothers. Where is André? The last we saw of him was a picture of you behind them, and a group of vampires behind you." That came out wrong. *Shit*. Before I can correct myself, Carlos cuts me off.

"Are you saying I had something to do with it?" Carlos's eyes flash with anger and turn a shade of ruby.

Ambroise growls out and his wings expand, covering me. "Watch how you speak to her. You know that isn't what she meant."

I rub Ambroise's wing and watch as they shiver, and his back relaxes. I can finally peek out from behind the winged curtain.

"Hey, look at me." Sofia grabs Carlos's face bring him down to her level. "Emotions are high right now. That isn't what she meant." She exhales as Carlos storms off to another corner. His fangs are out, and his eyes are sprouting veins again. "After we exchanged a few choice words between everyone," Sofia began, "we were headed back to your place." Her fingers played with her short black hair, snagging on the tiny knots. Her emerald-green eyes became glassy, and my heart hammered in fear of what she would say next. "They came out of nowhere. We did our best, but André shoved me into Carlos and told him to run. So, he did. He tossed me over his shoulder and ran. I don't know if he's alive or not. We came here to find Amélie and Javier to make sure they were okay."

Everyone gathered around the counter, hovering over my shoulder, staring at the screen.

"Can you all take a step back, please?" I know they're my family, but fucking hell, I can't breathe with them crowding over me. Ambroise presses a kiss to my temple and leans against the counter, his tail flicking at everyone's legs until they all give me some space. "This is where I traced Marcus's phone." We all knew what happened at the abandoned flour mill, but there were no reports of Marcus being there. "This is our best shot. If they have André, this is where they're keeping him."

"If he's still alive, you mean." Carlos lets out a humourless laugh. "You don't know the monster Marcus is."

"Oh? I don't?" I say, remembering every ounce of pain inflicted on me. Remembering every time I called my brother in secret and met up with him for a full year of me being undercover and begging him to let me leave. Carlos hangs his head. "¿Te da verguenza? Because you should be embarrassed. Just because we experienced different pain, doesn't mean the same monster didn't inflict it."

It's been two hours of Carlos and Ambroise butting heads with Amélie trying to placate both of them. Her frustration is rising faster than the rising tides. All they can agree on is Sofia and I are to stay here... where it's safe.

"You're going to sneak in there, right?" Sofia whispers to me.

The flipping of pages does a horrible job of masking Javier's eavesdropping. I hold one finger up to her. "Psst. Mira, chismoso, get over here." He cocks his head to the side, knowing I caught him.

"Sofia, what you're suggesting is a terrible idea." Javier slides the book across the counter.

"Javier." She says in a mocking tone. "I've never had a good idea a day in my life."

That's alarming. At least she's honest. Snatching the discarded book, my fingers flip through pages of herbs. Listening to ideas sprouting from my brother and my mate, I come up with one of my own. Turning my back on them, I grab hold of Javier's shirt, bringing him closer to me and Sofia. "I have an idea. It has the potential to go south really quick, but combined with their all-brawn tactic, it might work." I spin the book to show where my thoughts are.

Javier looks over his shoulder and Amélie is staring right at him, an indiscernible look on her face. Those black eyes dart over to me and pin me in place as she bores into my soul. *This is getting uncomfortable.* She smirks and nods. "This plan." She taps a paper with scribblings in all shades of ink. "This is the plan we will go with. It combines both of yours into one, so if anything goes wrong, you're both to blame." Her eyes lift from the paper and land on me. "Maybe if we add some lady luck, it'll work. Now, let's go get everything we need to save André."

The gargoyles have gone with Sofia and Carlos to the coven. Javier and I are in the back of Bound. The magical wards hum and buzz around us. Javier looks exhausted and hungry from placing so many. It was the only idea we had to get Ambroise and Carlos to leave.

"I don't like this, Vali." Javier says muddling herbs in between bites of trail mix that's more candy than nuts.

"We don't have a choice. No one knows Marcus the way I do. He won't stop until he has me." I gag as I pour the thick crimson liquid into a container. "I'm going to give Marcus exactly what he wants."

15

Ambroise

The coven denied any magical help, stating their fighters were away on other business. It's settled, I'm retiring.

"You know," Carlos begins as we drive back to Bound. "You don't look tan feo with that glamour. You should wear it more often."

"Snapping your neck would be like breaking a toothpick. You know this, right?" I pull at the collar of my sweater.

"Of course I do. Have fun explaining it to Val." He winks at me through the rearview mirror.

Smug son of a bitch.

I wrap Vali in my arms and kiss the breath out of her. I just found her and I'm afraid to lose her. "Promise me you'll stay here. No matter what happens."

"I'll stay here." She grabs my face and kisses me like her life depends on it.

Digging my fingers through her hair, I bring her closer, and she melts against me. I nibble on her bottom lip, she moans so sweetly, and I want more. My hands have a mind of their own as they wander over her frame.

"Hey! Stop corrupting my sister! I don't need to see that." Carlos shouts as he's saying goodbye to Sofia.

Javier groans readjusting the straps on the bag filled with magic-infused items and tonics in case we need them. "Now you know I feel."

Vali rests her forehead between my collar and jaw, and I move to leave a kiss there. "I'll see you soon." I whisper into her ear, and she nods while biting her lip.

As we pile into the car, I can't help but focus on the nagging feeling in my stomach. I only wish I knew what it meant.

Halfway to our destination Carlos laughs.

"What's so funny?" I ask from the back seat.

"She never actually promised." He says in laughter.

"She wouldn't." *Would she?* My statement pulls a roaring laughter from Carlos.

It's empty and quiet and I don't like it. It feels wrong. Clanking from the rafters overhead grabs our attention, but as we look, there's nothing there. Nodding to Amélie, we strip off our glamour and change, shoving our human clothing into the bag. She grabs Javier tightly and takes flight. Carlos and

I split up to cover more ground, but always staying within earshot of everyone. Going up a stairwell, grunts and the sounds of metal clanging whispers around me. Rushing up the stairs, I rip a door off the hinges and find André.

Two vampires ripped to shreds are the first thing to greet me. André's chest is heaving as he snaps the back of a third over his knee. He may be the charmer, but when he's fighting, he's more frightening than any monster under the bed. A roar shakes the ground, sparks fly off the tip of his claws as he gouges the cement wall.

"Frère, it's me." I raise my hands up, showing him I mean no harm. "Are you hurt?" Wind rushes around me as he flaps his wings over and over, calming himself.

"I'm okay." He tries to assure me with a gravelly tone. "If you don't tear that bâtard apart, I will." It's then I notice the wounds slowly healing. There's a sizeable hole in his right wing, tiny cuts litter his body where every vital vein and artery are.

"We'll do it together." I reassure him as the seed of hatred roots itself in me. *Marcus has many sins to atone for.* We share a moment of peace before the sounds of combat surround us.

"Amélie?" André asks.

"With Javier." The corners of my lips curl into a smile. "And Carlos."

André rolls his head. "I don't like him. He's bullheaded."

The moon began to rise. Dirt-stained windows diffused the silver beams lighting our way. Skittering noises up the walls and across the floors have us on high alert. Figures dart in and out of the shadows. "How about a little more light?" Javier asks, as he presses his palms together before pulling them apart. Yellow iridescent light pulses before expanding and shooting up towards the ceiling. This new light is almost as intense as the sun.

Carlos flinches and digs sunglasses out of his jacket. "You said a *little* more light."

These vampires are swarming out of everywhere and nowhere. We started out fighting side by side, but now we have been pushed to different corners. Screams and shouts become the haunting music for what should be a peaceful night. Amélie soars higher towards the yellow rafters, holding a vampire by his shoulders before she rips him in half with her talons, letting his carcass crash to the floor. She barrel-dives back into the crowd, leaving severed heads in her wake. André is covered in congealed blood as he throws bodies against the wall and punching through others with precision, tearing their hearts out and crushing them before their eyes. Carlos surprised me, having never gone into battle with him, his new-found vampire speed and strength worked to his tactical advantage. He moved with stealth and skill, severing spinal cords with his bare hands and ripping throats out with his teeth. Not too far from me, an explosion of light consumes a good fourth of the vampiric crowd. Bodies collapse and writhe as they burn. Javier blinks away his temporary blindness while wiping away the blood from his brow.

Bringing my wings in tight to my back, my heavy tail whips at two vampires, beheading them before I coil it back and plunge into the chest of another. All I see is red. None of these vampires are the man I came to end.

"Marcus!" I shout. He's a damn coward to hide behind so many. These are all either new or drugged out of their minds. Their movements are sloppy, and they should be faster than this. One vampire attempts to tackle me to the ground, with one swift kick I feel the pop of their knee beneath my foot, and they cry in pain. There's a moment where I can catch my breath and I glimpse my siblings fighting back- to-back, leaving a path of destruction while Javier and Carlos tag team the crowd in their corner.

There's a creaking sound behind me, followed by a rush of frigid air. Pain laces the back of my knee and ankle. Cold, heavy chains wrap around me, stunting my movements. Multiple points of pain pierce my neck and my body feels heavy. The chains pull tighter, biting into my flesh while a wave of vampires yank me to the ground.

"Frère!" I hear André and Amélie shout for me as the world turns black.

16

MARCUS

As I hoped, Carlos led me to Celia. What I hadn't expected was her being surrounded by those fucking gargoyles. Words don't exist for what I felt after my scouts mentioned one of them was her mate. They couldn't determine which one, since she was always with one or more of them. But that's fine. I'll slit their throats in front of her, then fuck her in the pool of their blood. She'll remember who she belongs to in no time.

The buzz from my phone bounces off the empty walls of this old factory, disrupting my meal. Tossing the now empty human to the ground, I stand and wipe the corner of my mouth. Savoring the last drop from the pad of my thumb, the bottom of my shoe catches on long red hair. A sneer surfaces on my face at the limp form, but morphs into a smile as I kick and watch her body skid along the floor. She could've been a permanent snack, but I want Celia to pick who we'll share after I turn her. Then we'll be a happy family.

The buzzing snares my attention again.

"What?" One of my men informs me my plan worked. We have all but one person Celia cares about. A smile splits my face, hearing the largest gargoyle is subdued and in chains. Ending the call, the smooth screen slides under my finger as I scroll through my gallery and land on a picture of Celia. I took this one in secret. Damn, she's sexy. Biting her lip and brows pinched as she stares at the tablet screen, worry engrained on her face. Soon, Celia. Soon that lip will mine to bite again.

"Wake up." My hand stings from the satisfying slap I gave the gargoyle my informants tell me is Ambroise. Chains rattle as he tries to stand. "Don't bother, those are thick enough to hold down a truck." Pacing the empty room, my fingers clutch the stack of photos from my pocket. Measured steps carry me closer to Ambroise as I shuffle each picture and toss them on the ground. They're close enough for him to see, but just out of reach. "Celia is beautiful. I can't wait to hear her voice and have her naked beneath me." The sad attempt to lunge at me pulls a cackle from the depths of me. "So, you're the one who's fucking her. It's okay. I won't punish her too harshly for allowing someone else to touch what is mine."

"She's my mate," He growls. Blood drips from my hands as my nails dig into my palms. "She'll never be yours or love you." Ambroise says. *He's so sure of himself.* Before this bastard can blink, I move in front of him and watch as his head snaps back with one perfectly placed hit to his nose.

Wiping my hands clean of the filth, I slip my phone out from my pocket.

I press my finger to my lips.

"Shhh. Look." I show him the camera feed on my phone. "She came to me, after all."

The chains rattle and creak as he fights harder against them. Chilled metal cuts into his skin. "Now now. Why don't you relax for a little while, and I'll go greet her." I know she isn't my beloved. I killed that one four years ago. That woman was insufferable so bold and noncompliant. But not my Celia. She's perfect. She's mine.

17

VALI

Ambroise is going to be pissed, but I'll deal with him later. Closing the door to Javier's 2013 Honda Civic, the door to the flour factory seems to shrink further into the distance. *This is going to work. It has to.* I didn't know a door could be so intimidating. I'm welcomed with bone-chilling silence. The scream never gets the chance to leave my lungs as a sour smelling rag smothers my mouth and nose, and chilly hands grab me.

There's a gentle caress on my cheek, but it makes my skin crawl.

"Celia, I missed you."

My eyes snap open.

"Marcus." His name tastes like sour milk. My body bends away from his as much as it can with him cuddling me on a couch. Wet kisses are dotted on my neck, and I realize that my coat, gloves, hat, and scarf are gone. I'm left in my cropped sweater, jeans, and boots. The cracked leather beneath me digs into my cheek. My skin is red, and it burns from the ropes around them being bound too tight. My fingers have gone numb. Doing my best; I squirm looking for anything to free myself, but I'm trapped under his heavy arm and draped leg over mine.

"If you're looking for all those pretty little knives you had tucked away." He runs his hand over my waist, and I feel the rising tide of vomit wash up my throat. "Those are safe somewhere else." *There goes plan b.* "Don't worry, though." He kisses and licks my neck, leaving a trail of disgust seeping into my pores. "We can play with them later." A small whimper leaves me as he nips my pulse point. "I knew you'd come home."

Remember the plan, Vali. Remember the plan. Find them first. Marcus slithers his hands over my breasts and tenderly massages them. Hot breath fans from the smile pressed at my neck down to my chest. My skin is crawling with how he gropes me. Everything about this is wrong. Pain digs into my jaw and the grinding of my teeth penetrates my ears as I clench my jaw, bracing myself. Stars burst behind my eyes as the back of my head collides with his iron jaw. With him stunned, I kick my legs as hard as I can. A weight is lifted off me after a dull thump in the open room. Jumping up from the couch, the room spins with the leftover effects of whatever they knocked me out with.

"Babe." Marcus's sinister chuckle tickles my nape as I run. "That wasn't very nice. I'm going to have to remind you of your manners."

Across the room, I spot shards of glass and B-Line it to my newfound saving grace.

"Come on." I beg the glass to cut faster and free me of the one thing still tying my fate to the monster hunting me. The glass does a great job of gouging my palms, as each strand of the rope is frayed one at a time. I'm running down a hallway as fast as my legs allow, my hands are free, but I'm not.

"Got you." His hand wraps around my throat. *Where the fuck did he come from?* "You really need to stop running from me." Marcus's nostrils flare as he inhales. Veins sprout around his eyes while those dark brown orbs now shine red. "Awe. Did you hurt yourself? You know I'm the only one allowed to hurt you."

I'm fighting for a single molecule of oxygen as I watch in horror. Marcus lifts my hand and licks me from elbow to fingertip. He goes back to the open cut in my palm and bites down and sucks harshly. My terror refuses to be caged and leaps from my lips in a shrill scream.

"I'm sorry! I'm sorry. I'm sorry. I'll be good." *Remember the plan, Vali. He has to believe this. Then find at least one of them. You can do this.*

He smiles up at me with stained lips and teeth.

"Yes, you will." He kisses his bite. "To make sure you behave, Celia." The look in his eyes dares me to correct him on my name, but I bite my tongue. "I'm going to take you to your mate and fuck you in front of him while he's helpless to do anything. Then I'm going to tear his head off and take you again as he showers us in his blood." Black spots crawl around the corner of my vision like an army of ants as he squeezes tighter.

"Don't you hurt him." I rasp out. My voice has turned gravely, and speaking is painful. But this pain wouldn't come close to losing Ambroise. "Don't you fucking hurt him." I claw at his hand and arm. He drops me like a sack of potatoes and I crash onto the cement floors. "I came to you, right? I'm here. Let him and everyone else go." A glass cylindrical tube presses into my hip. *Thank goodness it isn't broken.*

His knuckles stroke my cheek the way a lover would, but I know this isn't love. I hate how tender he's trying to be. "I could. But that isn't fun for me. Plus, you still need to learn your lesson." Marcus grabs a fistful of my hair and drags me across the floor and into another room.

My scalp is beyond the point of being tender. My jeans are covered in dirt and grime, while dry tears mar my cheeks.

"Ambroise." My gargoyle is bound to the ground with several thick chains. His eyes bolt open.

"Amourouse." His voice is thick with worry.

"My beautiful Celia." Marcus pulls me up and presses me to his chest.

The rivers of hell aren't hot enough to burn away his lingering touch. *This is close enough to the plan.* I can't stand his touch or hearing him call me that name anymore. "My name isn't Celia." It's the final nail in the coffin.

18

Vali

"Celia, Lola, Valeria, whoever you want to pretend to be, doesn't matter. Hell, you can be someone new every day of the week. Keep things fun and exciting. Because you are mine, and only mine." He clutches more of my hair. The strands rip out, the pain pricks my eyes, but I refuse to give him the satisfaction of seeing tears fall.

"Please, Marcus, let them go. You win, okay?" My voice cracks at the end and I hate it. "You win. If you let them all walk out of here alive, and don't try to find them ever again." His eyes narrow on me as he listens to my bargaining plea. "I'll be whoever or whatever you want me to be. It'll be just us, and we can go anywhere."

"You're giving in already?" His saccharine smile frames his fangs glinting in the low light. Readjusting his fingers, he pulls harder at my roots and pouts when he sees me wince. "I thought you were a fighter." The vein in Marcus's forehead throbs as he speaks through clenched teeth.

"Fighting looks different to everyone, Marcus." I gulp down the pain. "They're my family. I love them."

A sting radiates across my face before the sound of the smack reaches my ears. His fingers dig into my cheeks as he brings my face closer to his. The concern in his eyes is a mockery of his actions.

"Look at what you made me do, babe." He brushes the hair off my face. "I'm your family. We're going to be our own happy family." His sandpaper lips cover mine and he slithers his tongue into mouth. Bile churns in my stomach and threatens to erupt. "You don't love them. You love me. Only me." He turns my face and runs his fangs over my pulse point. "Say it. Say you only love me." Marcus digs his fingers into my cheeks harsh enough to spread pain across my jaw.

My eyes lock on Ambroise, and it breaks my heart. He's struggling against the chains. My gargoyle thinks he's failed me. Still looking at the perfect man in front of me, I smile. "I love you."

Ambroise's eyes track my hand as I slip a tiny vial out from the waistband and pour the contents into my mouth. Whipping my head to the side, I crash my lips against Marcus's, thrusting my tongue and the poison into his mouth. He drops me to the ground as he spits and claws at his mouth and neck. The ground ripples like waves, staggering my run until I crash against the graphite chest of my gargoyle and the chains dig into my chest.

There are several locks on them and now I'm really wishing I had learned to pick locks. I can feel the effects of the poison I concocted set in. My lips tingle, my tongue and throat burn. Breathing is a word I don't know the meaning of. Everything in me itches. Cold links bite into my palms as I pull harder, trying to detach them from him and the ground. Everything blurs in and out of focus around me, churning my stomach. Neon halos surround the light sources in the room.

"Vali, what did you take? Stop tugging the chains and look at me, amoureuse." The gentle command in his voice halts my movements, allowing the guilt to creep in.

"I made a poison with different ingredients I read about. Bound is a great resource. Who knew books could be so helpful, right?" I suck at trying to make light of a situation. "I need to get you out of these so we can find Javier. He has the antidote. Sofia has it too, but she's back at Bound. If it's the worst case, you'll need to fly me to her. So, no. I won't stop tugging on these chains." I rasp.

The doors burst open and more vampires flood space. My heart is lodged in my throat and pounding in my ears. A deep feral roar that shakes the walls rips from Ambroise. Metal creaks and clanks as his wings strain each link. The pattern of the chain embeds into his skin as his muscles bulge against them. Chains crash to the floor and I notice his one wing doesn't fully expand. It's broken and torn. "Vali, move." Ambroise shoves me behind him as Marcus launches himself at us.

Deep scratches line half of Marcus's face while plum and ruby veins burst under his skin. Did I mention how much I hate using poisons? His face, the way he moves, and breathes... Marcus is my nightmare incarnate.

Bursts of light filter from behind the crowd of vampires, sending them sailing through the air. Javier, Carlos, André, and Amélie. They all look tired and furious. If I didn't know they were on our side, I would be shitting bricks right now. The gargoyles flex their claws as they stalk into the room, tearing apart anyone who gets close to them. Carlos is the definition of the quiet before the storm. His eyes dart around the room before his lips curl into a snarl. Blackened veins web around his eyes before he punches into the chest of another vampire. The heart is still beating as he pulls his fist out, squeezing it like a sponge. He moves so fast I can't track him and the room turns into a horror filled merry-go-round.

While my new family makes quick work of the vampires, Ambroise busies himself with Marcus as Carlos and Javier step closer to me. My chest hurts, my arm is numb, and my breathing is shallow. *I guess oxygen isn't overrated.* Carlos grabs my face and it's odd seeing his eyes with a red hue. "You survived the chancla, a hunting knife, and you're going to survive this, too. You hear me? I can't believe you poisoned yourself." Before I can reply, he grabs me close and spins before a vampire can grab hold of me. His boot crushes the skull of the one who tried to grab me and thick ruby blood splatters on my leg.

"Carajo, Javier! Her pupils are blown out, and she's sweating. Muevete!"

The sound of ripping fabric barely registers as frantic footsteps filter from the right. Javier runs up to me after digging into one of his pockets.

"You better drink all of this." He tips my head back, and the hot purple liquid burns on my tongue before freezing in my throat. I'm choking and there's nothing I can do. The unwelcoming feeling of death's passionless kiss is on my neck. "Vali, you're okay. Keep swallowing. It's almost done." My throat fights against the antidote, gargling every forced gulp. Wet coughs erupt from me with the last drop. Uncontrollable dry heaving churns my stomach as I sag against my brother. Carlos holds me up and pushes my face into his chest, shielding me from the surrounding horrors. "That's only the first dose. We need to get you out of here so you can drink the rest." Javier says, before using magic to shield us. The vampires bounce off the invisible wall, but they won't stop crashing against it like waves on a rocky shore. Javier is sweating and his knees are buckling.

The gold handle of the hunting knife poking out of Carlos's waist screams for my attention against the dark clothing. I remember that knife. Even in this antidote daze, I can feel the blade being stuck in me again. All the horrors of that night flood into my mind like a tsunami. Tearing myself from my brother, I bring the knife with me. The shield dissipates with a fresh wave, and I run. Carlos's screams drift away in the sea of grunts and snapping bones. Ambroise senses me approaching. His broken wing popped out of place and resembles a cheese cloth from the abuse of the wall of vampires climbing on his back.

Marcus is barely recognizable, with his face coated in every shade of blood. The poison made him sluggish and painted his skin a dull shade of grey. There're gashes lining his right thigh as viscous blood pours out. Bodies are flown in every direction and an uppercut from Ambroise crashes Marcus into the ceiling. Cement and metal debris flurries to the surrounding ground, creating a grotesque snow globe with us in the center.

Staggering closer to Ambroise, he notices the knife in my hand glinting in the moonlight. With one hand, Ambroise lifts Marcus into the air and slams him into the cement pillar. His hand clamps around Marcus's throat, letting his claws pierce the skin beneath them. He nods, knowing what I have planned. Exhaustion is wrapping me in its embrace, but I'm not ready to give in yet. Kicking chunks of metal pipes out my way and stepping over corpses, I trudge closer to the man I hate with my entire being and to the man I love more than anything.

A sadistic laugh chills the air.

"What are you going to do, babe?" I never liked the endearment of babe, but I absolutely loath it after him. "You're just like me. You'd do anything to have what you desire. We deserve each other." He coughs and gasps, trying to free himself from a stone grip. "Stab him in the back, like you did to me."

Ambroise squeezes tighter, and Marcus's eyes bulge as veins burst under his skin.

"Amoureuse." He beckons me over, his tail flicking from left to right. Even though he doesn't want me near Marcus, he's giving me something priceless.

It's hard to decipher, which is burning hotter. The gold handle my fingers melt around, or the fury searing my veins. Whichever it is, I'll use it as fuel. Boiling blood thrums in my body, flooding my ears and vision, drowning out the world around me. All I can see is Ambroise and that hijo de la gran puta Marcus, who's pressed against the wall, feet dangling, and smiling like some kind of deranged rag doll. There are plenty of things I want to tell him. How I'm nothing like him, how he's a sadistic bastard, how I hope he rots in hell. But that would gift him more of my time, energy, and mind. Marcus doesn't deserve anymore of me.

Remembering all the times he inflicted pain on me for his own amusement, what he did to my brother, what he did to my mate, rage blinds me. Glinting metal enters my line of sight as I slash the blade across Marcus's chest. As the crimson viscous liquid drips down, it drains the smile from his face. One, three, seven more gashes, one right after the other, have painted my vision and face red, and I lose count. Precision is no longer important. Tattered skin hangs on to his body by mere threads of tissue. Muscle falls by the chunk. The burn on my muscles overpowers the burn in my blood. Lifting the knife over my head, I release my own brutal yell, driving it down into his heart. Over and over and over again until I'm following the corpse to the ground.

Strong arms wrap around my shoulders and chest. The feeling of safety washing over me, and I know it's Ambroise. "Shhhh, it's okay. You did it, Vali, you did it, amoureuse." *When did he stop holding Marcus?*

It isn't until he speaks my own pained screams and sobs enter my ears. Everyone else is silent. The last of our grotesque snow globe has fallen and settled. Vacant red tinted eyes stare up at me. When does the feeling of glory and victory set in? I'm numb. Is this shock or exhaustion? I'll chalk it up to the poison still brewing in me.

"Let's go home." Ambroise whispers into my hair.

I let him help me stand and the hiss escaping him isn't lost on me.

"Ambroise." My boots squeak as I turn to face him. His long black hair is a tangled mess, gouges litter his chest, but his wing looks painfully broken. A flicker from the embers of settled anger sets a tiny fire in me. Nodding and biting my lip, the bloody hunting knife taps against my thigh. Before Ambroise can say or react to the movement of me turning, the blade slices into the air. The wobble of the gold handle sticking out of Marcus's neck is the only sound filling the room. "Now we can go."

André and Amélie step next to Ambroise, each supporting one side of him. "Well, help fly you home." Amélie says shifting carefully around his battered wing. "The bag holding our glamour items went up in flames." She gives a small laugh and winks at Javier.

He scratches the back of his neck. "It was an accident."

"I appreciate you saving me." She offers him a soft smile. "Still, we're a bit big to fit into a car like this."

"Which home?" André asks with a stupid, sly smirk on his face.

Three gargoyles turn and stare with hopeful expressions. It's my choice, but they're wishing for one answer.

It's not like everyone had to give me puppy eyes. "Mine. Ours." I wipe my face with the only clean part of my sleeve. "If that's okay." Looking up, a heated blush breaks through the red stains on my face. Ambroise has no right to have that panty-melting grin on his face right now. How can someone look this handsome and sexy while injured?

"It's the only home I want." His deep voice chuckles out. "But... I don't really want to be apart from you right now."

A throat clears somewhere in the back of the room. "She can ride with one of us. We should get there around the same time." Carlos leans against the wall, staring at Javier. "Probably before." He says with a grin, knowing Sofia is there waiting for us.

"I don't want to think about you and my sister." He shuffles over to a smaller bag that was dropped during the fight, rifling through the contents. "Here," Javier holds up a jar with thick teal goo. "This will help speed up the recovery process. You have to drink it. Sofia's creation."

Ambroise's eyes go wide. "I think I'd rather stay injured."

"Ambroise." I scold, as I playfully slap his chest.

"Ow." He chuckles and rubs at the injury, "Okay, okay."

The moon is high, the air is cold, and I'm ready to go home. Carlos and Javier are waiting by the car and Ambroise's siblings are with them discussing who is going to come back and handle cleaning up this mess. From the sounds of it, Sofia has been volunteered. All of them are injured in some capacity, but Ambroise is the worst off. My focus is on toying with his fingers and claws. I don't want him to see the worry etched on my face. "I'll see you soon, okay? Be careful up there." I rock on my heels.

His claw traces a line down my cheek to under my chin, sending delicious shivers down my spine and raising goosebumps on my skin.

"Don't worry about me. My wing is feeling better already. See?" A gentle breeze covers me as his wing moves. He places a kiss on my forehead, nose, then lips.

"I'll see you at home." I brush my fingers over his cheek.

"Promise?" He arches his brow.

Butterflies don't even compare to the zoo he's unleashed stampeding in my stomach with that stare. "Promise."

19

Vali

Snow is falling outside again. The voices and music playing become white noise. It's Christmas Eve and two days since Marcus. Ambroise's injuries were more severe than we anticipated. He had no choice but to go into his stone form to recover. He hasn't broken out yet. I've also been on bedrest after consuming the poison. The antidote ended today. Now I play the waiting game to see what lasting effects there are. For now, I'm letting everyone make my home their own, partly because I have no desire to ask them to leave, and because they refused to leave me and Ambroise. Rolling over the sheets tangle between my legs as I reach for my gargoyle. Tracing the stone angles of his face, I send a Christmas wish to anyone who may be listening of wanting to swim in those onyx pools again.

"Please get better soon." I whisper. A knock on the door grabs my attention.

"Hey Val." Carlos pokes his head in. The aroma of arroz con gandules and pernil invades my nostrils and has me salivating. He walks in and quickly shuts the door with his foot. "Sofia is going to be pissed if she sees me feeding you actual food and not that bullshit broth she's been making you drink."

"Pretty sure that bullshit broth is magic medicine." Pushing myself up higher on the bed, I smile and wiggle as I grab the plate while he holds a drink. I shove a generous amount of food into my mouth. The flavors of my childhood burst on my tongue and warm both my stomach and soul. I'm so glad they let me out of bed to make this. I've seen how they all cook. It's either burnt, or a dick is near it. "Thank you. I was ready to give her full access to all my computer systems and help her stalk her favorite celebrity, if it meant I could eat solid food." My toes wiggle as I eat, and I grin as a devious thought comes to mind. "If I told her what you said, what would she think?"

"Don't you dare tell her. She's already a brat. I don't need her nagging too." I smack his hand as he tries to steal a piece of pork off my plate.

Grabbing the glass from him and downing a sip of coquito, an uncontrollable cough surfaces. "Woo. That's a lot of rum." I bring the chilled glass up to my lips and take another small sip.

"André made it under Javier's supervision. We almost fought when they tried to make it with eggs." Carlos laughs and I can't help but join him. "How would you feel about me moving here?" The foot of my bed dips as he sprawls out. "André suggested merging our businesses. He tells me you've been building a new information collection system on us supernatural beings."

Damn, I guess I am the odd one out. "I would love all of that. I bet Sofia would too."

He stayed with me while I finished, so he could sneak the evidence back out. He leaves the door ajar in case I need anything.

"Carlos, what did you take in there?" Sofia's angry tone causes me to chuckle.

"Listen, chiquitita." There's a bit of panic in Carlos's voice. "I swear I didn't do anything."

The heavy footsteps and laughter help to make this home. "They make a cute couple, don't they?" I ask Ambroise as my eyes flutter close.

20

AMBROISE

Three hours I've sat here watching her sleep. Dark circles line her eyes and guilt slithers in me, knowing it's because of me. I listened to her ramblings. She's barely slept. Vali's lips are soft and warm against mine as I brush them with a kiss. The night is silent, and the dim lighting only adds to the beauty of her eyes fluttering open.

"Merry Christmas, amoureuse." I whisper.

Her eyes fly open and arms fling around my neck before she smashes her lips against mine and we're consumed in a clash of lips, teeth, and tongues. "Merry Christmas." Her smile is breathtaking.

"I'm so happy you're okay." I place a kiss on her forehead. It's only been a few days, and my need for her is insurmountable. I have to have her now.

My claws drag torturously as they rip on a single tear down the red silk pajamas that barely reach her thighs. They fall open and I finish ripping them off and push her onto her back. "Look at you," I massage her thighs, "the perfect present laid out for me." She surprises me by hooking her legs around my waist and flipping us so she's on top of me.

Her hands rove over me, touching and exploring every inch. A smirk appears as she finds my hardened cock. "Fuck, Vali." My head leans back as I savor her touch. The need for her is indescribable. "Tonight, you're going to take my knot." Vali's hand stills over my ridges and I can hear her heart ramming against her ribs. It excites me more, and precum leaks from me. The bed dips as I switch our positions. Kissing down her neck, I grab hold of her breasts, enjoying the full weight of them, and continue my trek down her body. Every stretch mark, dimple, and curve is lavished with attention. Dragging my claws down, she shivers, and I smile. I've barely touched her, and she's already wet. Using the heel of my palm, I push against her core, and she grinds against me. "Just like that, amoureuse. Make yourself come on my hand."

The sheets crumple as she grips them while she writhes and grinds harder. I add in small licks to her clit, loving how sweet she tastes until she comes apart in my hand. Sitting back, I look at her. "Open your eyes." When she does, I keep my gaze on her as I lick my hand clean and groan in pleasure. "Damn, you're so sweet."

"Ambroise." She whimpers. My eyes track her hands as she plays with her ample breasts.

Placing my weight on my forearms, I hook her legs over my arms and give her no warning as I thrust into her. Vali screams out my name again and tugs harshly at her nipples. Slowly, I slide back out.

"You take me so well." I grunt out before ramming back into her. *Fuck, I love how she grips me.* Going faster, her hand snakes between us and she rubs short, hard circles over her sensitive nub. The moans from her lips encourage me to piston my hips faster and harder. I can feel my knot slipping in as she lifts her hips to meet my thrusts.

"I'm going to come." Vali pants and her walls suck me in deeper. Her orgasm rips through her. Thighs quiver around my arms as she gushes and squirts on me. Witnessing her fall apart for me with tousled hair, a flush deepening her bronze skin, and breasts bouncing with each labored breath, calls to a primal part in me.

Dropping one of her legs and hitching the other higher to my shoulder, I find her soft spot where her shoulder meets her neck. Careful of my claws, I wrap my hand around that spot and stroke her jaw with my thumb before I thrust hard. The banging of the headboard is the harmony to the melody of her screams and moans. Keeping pace, I'm hypnotized by her face, sculpted with pleasure. I'm falling deeper in love with this woman.

"You're going to take everything I give you, and I'm going to fill you with my cum until I'm dripping out of that pretty pussy." My tail vibrates around the opening her ass before slipping in.

Her lips land on my wrist as she plants fervent kisses.

"Yes, Ambroise! I want it. I need your cum in me."

A deep roar rumbles the bed as my knot pushes into her. I spill in her as I rock my hips. She clenches around me and trickles of cum drip as I continue to fill her. The way her eyes roll back is only helping me spill into her more. We're both slick with sweat, trying to catch our breath. Her skin is hot under my lips as I kiss my way up her stomach to her neck, jaw, and lips. I gently place her other leg on the bed and wrap her in my arms as I turn us over so she can rest on me.

She snuggles into my neck and wiggles her hips as I wrap my wings around us. "Stop moving like that, or else my knot will never go away." I chuckle.

"You say that like it's a bad thing." She giggles. We're lost in a haze of laughter, love, and lust as we hold each other.

Fifteen minutes later and I'm still in heaven. She's snoring on my chest and there's a pool of drool forming on my chest. *Still beautiful.* Pushing the hair off her face, I kiss her head.

"Vali." She groans, asking for five more minutes. I wait twenty more before waking her with gentle touches and kisses. "Amoureuse, let me clean you up." Vali nods, wiping the drool and sleep away from her face. "I love you."

"I love you, too." She says with a smile.

Her smile is a thief. It's stolen my breath, heart, and world. She can keep them.

21

VALI

Here's a sight I will never tire of seeing.

"I didn't get you anything," I say as Ambroise walks towards the bed in all his naked glory.

The soft sheets caress my skin as he slides in next to me, pressing my back against his front. His wing covers me in place of the blanket. He's the greatest feeling in the world.

"What we just did is a perfect present." He chuckles into my hair. "I have you. It's all I'll ever need." The emerald sheets gather at my feet as I move to lie on my side and face him. "If it makes you feel better, I didn't get you anything either."

My fingers draw random shapes up and down my gargoyle's arm.

"You've already given me everything." The velvet texture of his wing brushes my back and thighs as he pulls me closer.

"As long as I'm able, I'll give you everything I can." His soft lips leave a warm kiss on my head.

"Hey, Ambroise?" He hums in response. "Are you immortal?"

"No. But I do have a longer natural life than you. Not that it matters." He says while running his fingers up and down my spine. Before I can ask how it doesn't matter, because it seems pretty important to me, he speaks. "After we are both old and have lived our lives to the fullest." He kisses my chin. "And if we have any children and they are all grown and no longer need us." One more kiss to my nose. "And if I should have the unfortunate fate of outliving you." He kisses my forehead. "I'll turn to stone for eternity and watch over you, wherever it is you lay." Ambroise leaves a feather light kiss on my lips, but I can feel the weight of his heart in it.

"Promise?" I whisper into his chest.

He gently grips my jaw, bringing my face closer to his. *God, I love him.* I could stare into his eyes all day.

"Promise. I love you, Vali."

"I love you, Ambroise." I lay there in bliss, feeling the rise and fall of his chest and his heart beneath my palm as the snow falls silently outside. This is the best Christmas, and my gargoyle is the best gift.

Afterword

Dear Reader,

I hope you enjoyed reading "The Gargoyles Gift" as much as I enjoyed creating it. This book had a full cast full of loveable and memorable characters and I promise, you haven't seen the last of them. Stories are planned for Amelie and Javier, Carlos and Sofia, as well as Andre with his own love interest.

Make sure you checkout my other works and sign up for my newsletter so you'll have the most up-to-date information on each story and when it's expected to release.

Also By

Marilu Moser

Fated Deals: The Reaper Tomes Novella 1
A New Era: The Reaper Tomes Book 1
Call of the Coven: The Reaper Tomes Book 2
[Releases in 2023]

Home Sweet Haunted Home

Acknowledgments

First, I want to thank my husband for supporting and validating my dreams of being an author. I would've never started any of this if it wasn't for his love, encouragement and support.

I'll be always thankful to the meaningful connections I made this year with so many authors in the Romance Riot. This group of amazingly talented writers gave me the push I needed to write the story I've always wanted, but always talked myself out of. Thank you to the awesome beta reading group who helped shape this story.

Thank you to my best friends Kevin, Andrew, Gloria, Katie, and Chris for not only supporting me, but also hyping up every story idea I have.

Thank you to my editor Samantha Swart, who polished this story and made it even better. You are truly talented and stuck with me.

To the ever-amazing Hypegirls at Hypegirl PA services, I appreciate you so much. This amazing group of ladies kept me on track and took the stress away from all the little things that bog me down and created more time for me to write this story and all my other future projects.

Last but certainly not least, thank you to the wonderful community across my social media platforms for supporting a dream.

About Author

Marilu Moser is a Latina Urban Fantasy author, born and raised in the state known for its chocolate, crayons, and Independence Day history, Pennsylvania. She is is a self proclaimed connoisseur of dad jokes and perpetual optimism with a weakness for root beer floats and pizza. When she's not creating worlds full of memorable characters, she enjoys losing herself in between the pages of other books curled up next to the two family dogs, binge-watching crime shows, playing with Hotwheels with her children, and winning every board game against her husband.

You can connect with her at www.marilumoser.com

Made in the USA
Coppell, TX
07 January 2023